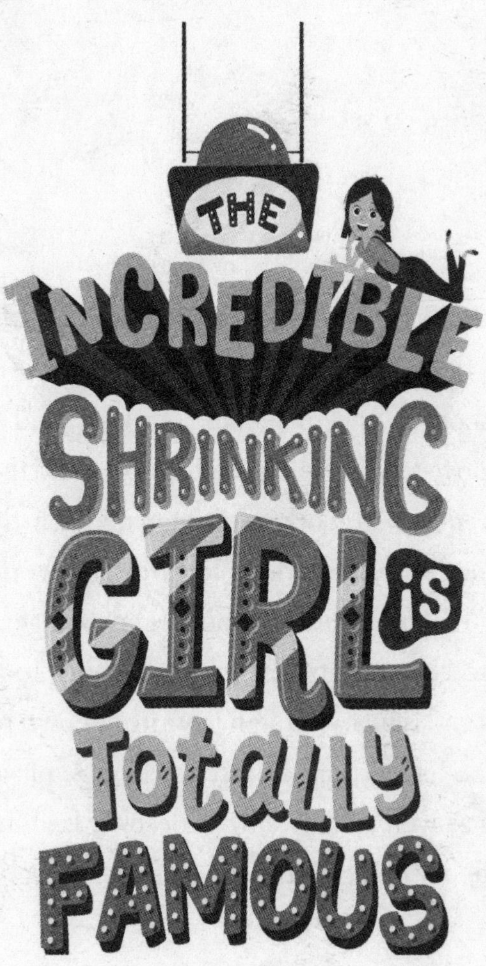
THE
INCREDIBLE
SHRINKING
GIRL is
Totally
FAMOUS

LOU KUENZLER was brought up on a remote sheep farm on the edge of Dartmoor. After a childhood of sheep, ponies, chickens and dogs, Lou moved to Northern Ireland to study theatre. She went on to work professionally as a theatre director, university drama lecturer and workshop leader in communities, schools and colleges. Lou now teaches adults and children how to write stories and is lucky enough to write her own books, too. She has written children's rhymes, plays and novels as well as stories for CBeebies. Lou lives in London with her family, two cats and a dog.

www.loukuenzler.com

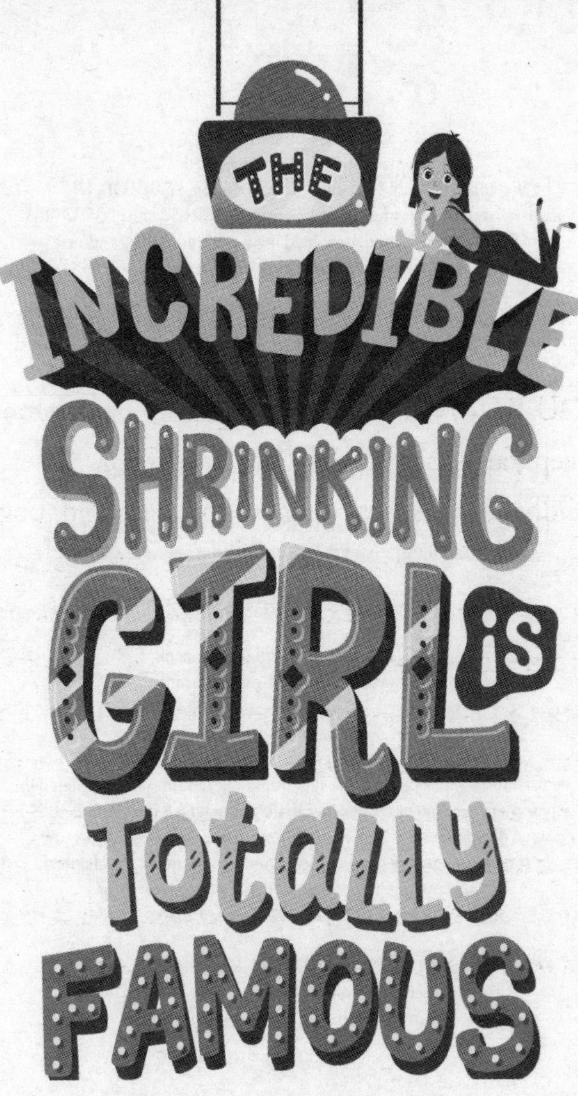

LOU KUENZLER

Illustrated by Kirsten Collier

SCHOLASTIC

Scholastic Children's Books
An imprint of Scholastic Ltd
Euston House, 24 Eversholt Street, London, NW1 1DB, UK
Registered office: Westfield Road, Southam, Warwickshire, CV47 0RA

First published in the UK as *Shrinking Violet Is Totally Famous*
by Scholastic Ltd, 2013
This edition published 2018

ISBN 978 1407 18781 5

A CIP catalogue record for this book
is available from the British Library.

Printed by CPI Group (UK) Ltd, Croydon, CR0 4YY
Papers used by Scholastic Children's Books are made
from wood grown in sustainable forests.

1 3 5 7 9 10 8 6 4 2

www.scholastic.co.uk

To Maureen –

the best childminder in the world. LK

My name is Violet Potts.

This story begins as I was slurping a totally delicious chocolate-fudge milkshake through a curly-whirly straw.

"Scrumdiddilyumptious!" I grinned.

"I made it just the way you like it," said Mo, the café owner, as she squashed past the back of my stool.

Mo had been busy with other customers when I first arrived. But the café was empty now. She flung her plump arms around me and **SQUEEZED** me so tightly I felt like one of the oranges in her fresh juice machine.

"It's lovely to see you," I wheezed.

I've known Mo ever since I was a tiny baby. She used to look after me and my sister, Tiffany, when we were both little. Then a few years ago, Mo gave up being a childminder and opened **UDDERLY PERFECT**, the best milkshake bar in the Whole Wide World, right here beside the community centre on the edge of King's Park.

"What've you been up to? I haven't seen you for ages," she said.

"Looking after Chip," I explained. Chip is my uncle's small shaggy dog, but he actually lives with us most of the time while Uncle Max travels abroad.

"You know dogs aren't allowed in the café," I said. "And Chip hates being tied up outside. . ."

"Health and safety," sighed Mo. "I can't afford to bend the rules. Not even for you, Violet. The council would love an excuse to close this place down. They want to build a multi-storey car park here, you know?"

"They can't do that!" I gasped.

Mo shrugged. "So *no* dogs . . . not even cute ones."

"Don't worry," I said. "Uncle Max is home at

the moment, so Chip is staying with him for three weeks . . . and I am making up for lost milkshake time." I ran my finger down the menu. "I think I'll try a Toffee Tornado Twirl next."

"That's a new flavour," said Mo. "I should give you a free sample, to see what you think."

"You *should*!" I agreed.

"But I can't," she said, shaking her head. "Your mum would tell me off. You know she doesn't like you to have too much sweet stuff. How about a fresh Carrot Juice Cooler instead?"

"A Carrot Juice Cooler? No way, Mo. Mum's not even here," I protested. "She's at work. Tiffany's looking after me. See?" I pointed out of the window. "She's babysitting little Rosie Johnson at the same time."

Tiffany, my terrible teenage sister, was lying on a bench sunbathing in the playground. She had her headphones in her ears and was flicking through a magazine while Rosie, the tearaway tot she was *supposed* to be watching, was trying to push a little boy off a swing.

Mo shook her head. "I've already made you two milkshakes as it is." She pointed to my chocolate shake and a Strawberry Shortbread Slurper on the counter beside it. "I bet that's not for Tiffany."

"It's for Nisha. We are going to play in the park," I explained. I was expecting my best friend any minute. Although I *was* thinking if she didn't get here soon, I might just try a TINY sip of Strawberry Slurper for myself. . .

"Nish'd better hurry up," laughed Mo, as if reading my thoughts.

"That's not fair," I cried. "I'd never touch a drop."

"Hmm," said Mo, heading back to the kitchen. She knows me *far* too well. The minute she was out of sight, I edged the strawberry milkshake towards me. But as I ***TILTED*** the straw forward, Nisha came tearing through the door, her long, black plaits flying behind her.

"Violet," she panted. "You've got to come. I ran all the way. . ."

Nish bent over double trying to breathe. "She's – **PUFF** – here – **PUFF**. . . Now – **PUFF**. . . Hurry. . ."

"Who's here?" I said, holding out the

Strawberry Slurper. "Take a sip of that and tell me slowly."

"Yum." Nish took the glass.

"Now start again," I said as she wiped away a thick pink milk-moustache with the back of her hand. "Who's here?"

"*STELLA* LIGHTFOOT," gulped Nisha.

"In the high street. I saw her. . ."

"*Stella Lightfoot?*" I almost dropped the last of my chocolate milkshake on the floor. "*The* Stella Lightfoot? Presenter of the best TV show in the Whole Entire Universe?"

"Yes!" Nisha jumped up and down.

"**EXPLORE GALORE!**" we both cried, just like Stella Lightfoot does when she leaps out of the helicopter at the beginning of every show. **EXPLORE GALORE!** is my absolute favourite television programme *ever*. Stella Lightfoot is the super-cool presenter who visits totally dangerous places, escapes ferocious animals and does super-daring stunts wherever she goes.

"What's Stella Lightfoot doing here in Swanchester?" I said, excitement swirling in my stomach like milkshake in a curly-whirly straw. "There aren't any charging rhinos on the high street, are there?" I wriggled on my stool, swinging my legs in the air. "Have killer sharks invaded the swimming pool. . .?"

"No, Stella's giving a talk at Pages Bookshop in half an hour," Nisha explained, "then signing copies of her new book all afternoon."

"Stella Lightfoot. At our local bookshop. I can't believe it," I cheered, pushing myself off from the counter so that my stool spun in a complete circle like a merry-go-round.

"I might actually get to meet my favourite telly star and . . . uh oh!" I felt a sudden DIZZY feeling in my head. I stretched out my hand to steady myself. But I knew it wasn't the spinning stool that had done it.

"What is it?" Nisha asked. "Violet? Are you all right?" She looked sideways at me. "Oh no! You're not going to. . ."

But it was too late. I felt a familiar tingling in my toes and. . .

WHOOSH!

"Look out, Nish! It's happening. I'm shrinking again," I cried.

I have shrunk quite a few times now – it happens whenever I get overexcited (and hearing Stella Lightfoot was in town was definitely exciting news). The tingling in my toes is always the first clue that I'm about to shrink. As soon as I felt it, I tucked my feet tight underneath me so I wouldn't fall off the stool.

"I'm so sorry," gasped Nisha, who knows all about my shrinking. "I should *never* have mentioned Stella Lightfoot. I should have known you might. . ."

"Too late," I squealed as I grabbed helplessly at the counter and sent both our milkshakes flying. The tickle in my toes shot up my legs. There was a fizzy feeling in my stomach, my ears popped and I shrank to the size of an apple core.

A giant tsunami of sticky milkshake WHOOSHED off the counter towards me. I clung to the seat of the red leather stool, almost swept away like a twig in the tide. As the wave passed over me, milkshake ran through my hair, and down my arms and legs.

Whenever I shrink, whatever I am wearing shrinks too. Since my shoes were now no bigger than apple pips, they quickly filled to the brim with thick chocolate and strawberry goo.

"Gross . . . but also a little bit delicious!" I giggled, licking my arm as I peered down over the edge of the stool.

Pink and brown milkshake was spattered across the floor. It was like one of those amazing, crazy paintings where the artist goes wild, throwing blobs of colour everywhere.

Luckily, neither of the glasses had broken and they clattered to a stop against the legs of a chair.

"What's going on out here?" said Mo, poking her head through the kitchen doorway.

It was lucky she had been in there all this time and didn't see me shrink.

"Oh. It's just you, Nish?" she said. There were still no other customers in the café. It must have looked as if Nisha was sitting all on her own. I was much shorter than the top of the counter now, so Mo had no idea I was crouched down there on the stool, dripping like a soggy biscuit.

"Where's Violet gone?" she asked, her hands on her hips. "And *WHAT* is all this mess?" Mo pointed at the sticky floor and walls.

"Er. . ." Nisha quickly threw a paper cow-print napkin over the top of my head to hide me. "Violet is. . . Well. . . Erm. . . We're really sorry, Mo. We had a bit of an accident," she blushed.

"I'll get a mop," said Mo. She clicked her

tongue – a sound I knew well from when I used to get into trouble as a little girl.

"Are you all right?" hissed Nisha, lifting up the napkin as soon as Mo turned back towards the kitchen.

"Yes," I said, making a mini thumbs-up sign.

Nisha bent low so she could hear my tiny voice.

"And I'm still desperate to see Stella Lightfoot," I said. "We have to get out of here. You know I can't let anybody see me once I've shrunk. Not even Mo."

Only two people in the entire world know about my special shrinking secret. Nisha found out when we visited a pet rescue centre recently. I got overexcited about the dogs and shrank right before her eyes. I should have known I couldn't hide anything from my best friend for long.

The only other person who knows is my grandma – she used to be a shrinker too when she was a girl. Gran's the one who told me the world isn't ready to share our LITTLE SECRET just yet . . . and the more times I shrink, the more I think she is right. People would either want to pickle me in a jar like a crazy science experiment, or worse, they'd want to tuck me up in a ball of cotton wool and never let me out in case I got hurt.

"Come on, Nish. Pop me in your pocket," I grinned. "Nothing is going to stop me seeing Stella Lightfoot up close and in real life."

"Really?" Nisha looked a bit worried. "I suppose my mum did say it would be OK for us to go to the bookshop. She called your mum when we saw Stella Lightfoot was going to be there and they agreed it would be all right as long as we stayed together."

"Exactly. And we *will* be together," I promised. "I'll be right inside your pocket."

I could hide there until I grew back to full size again. I never know how long my shrinking is going to last. I might even be big again by the time we got to the bookshop.

"Come on then," said Nisha. "I saw Tiffany in the sandpit. I'll tell her where we're going." She picked me up with the edge of the cow-print napkin. "But you can stay wrapped up in that. I don't want everything getting sticky from the milkshake."

She dropped me into the small side pocket of her yellow summery dress.

"Yippee!" I kicked my foot three times to tap Nisha's leg. I hoped she would understand that we needed to move *FAST*. I felt terrible about leaving Mo to mop up the spilt milkshake but I didn't want her to ask Nish too many questions about why I had suddenly disappeared. Not when we needed to get to the bookshop as quickly as we could. Nisha charged towards the door of **UDDERLY PERFECT**.

Suddenly she lurched sideways. "Oh, sorry, sir. Excuse me," she said.

I peeped out of her pocket and saw she had nearly collided with a tall, skinny man with a moustache like a bristly toothbrush. He was clutching a clipboard and wearing a long, clean, white coat and white Wellington boots.

"Look where you're going, young lady," he said as Nisha dodged past him in the doorway.

"Sorry," she called, running on.

But as we charged down the path, a terrible CRASH came from inside the café.

"Ahhhh!" Thud.

It sounded as if the white-coat man had slipped on something and a stool had been knocked over.

Nisha stopped running.

Oh no! The spilt milkshake, I thought. *We really should have cleaned it up*.

"What should we do, Violet?" Nisha hissed.

"Steady, sir." I heard Mo's warm, comforting voice drift out through the open window.

"This place is a death trap," snapped the man. He sounded furious . . . but at least that meant he was OK.

"Go!" I kicked my foot against Nisha's leg again. Mo would look after Mr White Coat. There was nothing we could do.

I must have kicked Nisha a *little* harder than I thought.

There was a horrible RIPPING sound. The seam of Nisha's pocket tore apart. Maybe my tiny feet are as sharp as pins. Or perhaps the cotton material of Nisha's summer dress was super-thin. . . The pocket flapped open like a trapdoor with nothing underneath it but an endless drop

DOWNWARDS. . .

"Nish! Stop!" I cried. But I knew it was hopeless. Nisha would never be able to hear my tiny voice.

I clung to the edge of the ripped pocket as she sped on again, but the thread was unravelling fast. I wriggled about, trying to get a better grip and swing myself up, away from the gaping hole. Nish must have thought I was still kicking her leg to run faster. She sped up even more. We were right in the middle of the playground now. Painted hopscotch squares flashed by underneath me as Nish sprinted along.

"I can't hold on much longer," I yelled hopelessly as the cow-print napkin flapped around my face.

"Hello, Tiffany," I heard Nish call above the noise of shouting children.

She slowed down for a moment.

"Hi, Nisha. Where's Violet?" answered Tiff.

"Er ... she's coming to Pages Bookshop with me. It's just down the high street," Nisha answered truthfully. "Stella Lightfoot is signing books. Your mum said we could go as long as we told you where we'd be."

"Fine," agreed Tiff. "I'm going to take little Rosie back to her house."

"My mum will pick us up later," called Nish as she **SWERVED** away across the edge of the sandpit. "See you soon, Tiffany – whoa!" Her foot caught in a bucket-shaped hole. I was thrown forward.

"Ahhhhh!"

Nish tripped and wobbled but she didn't fall. It was too late for me, though ... the fraying cotton of her pocket slipped between my fingers. I dangled for one last moment like a spider hanging from a thread, and then I PLUNGED through the hole and out the bottom of her dress.

"Help!"

I landed with a soft thump on the sand below. I poked my head out from underneath the cow-print napkin.

Nisha steadied herself and ran on.

"Bye, Tiffany," she called, *SPEEDING AWAY* towards the bookshop.

She had NO idea that she had left me behind.

"Nish, come back."

I blinked as I peered across the sandpit from under the napkin.

"Yuck!" All the bits of me that had been covered in milkshake had a GRITTY, STICKY layer of sand stuck on the top now. I felt like a lollipop that had been dropped on the ground.

Nisha will stop in a second, I thought, squinting as she sped away, weaving between toddlers building sandcastles in the bright sunshine. *She'll feel that I'm not in her pocket and come running back.*

If I'd been big, I could have caught up with her in two minutes flat. Now that I had shrunk, the sandpit at King's Park might as well have been the vast Sahara Desert for the distance there was between us. I stared helplessly across the hot sand as she headed for the park gate and the high street beyond.

I'll never catch up with her while I'm tiny, I thought, fanning my face with the edge of the napkin. *How will I get all the way to Pages Bookshop to see Stella Lightfoot without Nisha's help?*

I brushed sticky sand out of my eyes. The sun was beating down and I was starting to sweat.

What would Stella Lightfoot do if she were stranded in the middle of a desert?

Easy. She'd lasso a wild camel and ride it. But

there weren't any camels in the sandpit. All I could see were stomping feet and ankles, as toddlers churned up the sand like runaway bulldozers or diggers with spades.

"Come on, Rosie," I heard Tiffany call, as her ankles came into view above me. "Time to go home."

I ducked sideways. If only Tiff was taking Rosie to the shops. I could leap on to the toddler's flowery pink sandals and hitch a ride. But Rosie lives in one of the big houses on Hill Street, which is in the completely opposite direction to the bookshop.

"I want to stay here," Rosie whined, flopping down on the sand. "I'm pretending to be a girl mermaid."

Somewhere right behind me, I heard the CRUNCH of a spade.

"Me make weally big sandcastle," said a dribbly voice, which sounded like it belonged to a little boy.

I FROZE, crouching under my napkin.

I'd been so busying watching Rosie and trying to figure out a plan to reach Stella Lightfoot, I'd ignored the danger I was in. A sandpit is a risky place if you're no bigger than an apple core.

"Me dig wight here!" said the dribbly voice.

There was a sharp scratching noise as the spade dug down just a millimetre behind me. It pushed deep into the sand, almost scraping my ankles. Still crouched under the grubby napkin, I could feel the back of my feet slipping away beneath me.

I toppled backwards. I just had time to grab the

edge of the napkin and pull it over my head again as the spade shot up into the air with me on board. For a moment, it felt as if I were in a super-fast lift, shooting to the top of a multi-storey building.

"Yuck!" I heard Rosie's voice as she came closer. "That napkin is dirty," she said, sounding very bossy. I couldn't see, but I imagined she probably had her hands on her hips, or was waggling her finger like a teacher.

"Drop it down, silly!" Rosie commanded.

"It's only wubbish!" said the dribbly voice. But the spade tipped. . .

"Wheeeeeeee!"

I flew through the air, my napkin billowing around me like a tiny superhero's cape.

FLUMP!

I landed face down in the sandpit again.

I lay still, trying to catch my breath. But I knew I should try and make a run for it.

THUD!

A spadeful of sand rained down on top of me.

If I moved, someone might see me. But if I stayed here, I'd be buried as if I were in a desert tomb.

I remembered the school project we did last term about Ancient Egypt. I did *not* want to be found under a giant pyramid of sand, all SHRIVELLED and DRIED like a miniature Egyptian mummy, wrapped up in cow-print napkin bandages.

Keep calm, I told myself.

"Stinky litter. Put it in the bin," said Rosie. She sounded as if she was almost on top of me. I could see the dark shadow of her fingers through the napkin. Her hand was just a centimetre away – like a GIANT GRABBER CLAW.

"Yucky. Dirty rubbish," she said.

Her grabber-claw fingers swooped down.

Yikes! I wanted to scream. But I lay as still as a teaspoon in a drawer, trying not to breathe.

It was no good – the minute she lifted the napkin, Rosie saw me.

"Tiffney! Tiffney!" she cried, pointing down at the sand. "Look. Someone has lost their teeny-tiny dolly."

"Really?" Tiffany sounded bored. I heard the SNAP of the little hand mirror she carries everywhere and guessed she was checking her lipstick. *This is it*, I thought as her shadow fell across me. No matter how still I lie or how tiny I am, Tiffany will recognize me straight away. I *am* her sister, after all. We share a bedroom, for goodness' sake. Even though Tiff spends about twenty-three and half hours a day staring at her own reflection, she must have looked at me long enough to know that Rosie's teeny-tiny lost dolly had *my* freckled face, *my* short, brown hair and. . .

PIP PIP . . . just at that second Tiffany got a text message.

"Hang on, Rosie. It's from my friend Monique," Tiff said. "I wonder what she wants?"

"What about the dolly?" whined Rosie.

"Keep it if you like," shrugged Tiffany. She was right above me, but I could see she was staring at her text without even glancing at the ground. "Things get lost and buried in the sandpit all the time."

"Goody!" cheered Rosie. Her hot, pink fingers closed around me and she lifted me up.

I lay as still as I could, pretending that I really was a lost toy.

Rosie opened her hand and looked at me.

"I am going to call you Princess Tiny-Twinkle-In-My-Pocket," she said, grinning down at me with a big gappy-toothed smile.

"That's a weally silly name," said the dribbly boy, leaning over her. He poked his finger at me. "She doesn't even look like a pwincess." He pulled at my brand new purple-and-black CAMOUFLAGE shorts. They are just like the ones that Stella Lightfoot wears. "These aren't pwincess clothes," he spat.

Rosie turned her back on him.

"You *are* a princess aren't you, dolly? You are Princess Tiny-Twinkle," she said, pulling me up to stand by the roots of my hair.

OUCH! I screamed inside my head. *THAT HURTS!*

"First I'm going to take you home," smiled Rosie. "Then I am going to give you a *total* princess makeover . . . with real glitter!"

As Rosie skipped across the sandpit, I risked glancing from side to side, desperately hoping to see Nisha. She must have reached the bookshop by now. As soon as she realized I was missing, she'd be sure to come back to the park to look for me. But there was no sign of her yet.

At this rate, I'd never escape from Rosie and I'd never get to see Stella Lightfoot. . .

At the edge of the sandpit, Tiffany was still texting on her phone.

Rosie stopped skipping and peered at me.

For a moment I thought she might have seen me blink. Her big blue eyes narrowed. "What's that?" she said, licking her finger. She rubbed at my freckles as though they were drawn on with pen and might come off if she scrubbed at them hard enough.

Then she puckered up her lips and planted a big wet kiss right on the end of my nose.

Yuck!

She smacked her lips together, ready to kiss me again.

I can't stand this, I thought, just as the dribbly boy ran over and grabbed me by my feet.

"Get off," cried Rosie.

"I weally want to look at her." Dribbles yanked hard on my ankles.

"NO!" Rosie held on by my hair.

The two of them PULLED AT ME like a tiny Christmas cracker.

"Hey!" At last Tiffany noticed them fighting and turned around. She must be the worst babysitter in the world.

"Stop that," she said. Tiff grabbed hold of me. She didn't look down but I was left dangling from her hand by one arm, my feet swinging in the air as if I were clinging to the monkey bars.

"Come on, Rosie," said Tiffany. "We're going home."

"But what about Princess Tiny-Twinkle? I want to carry her," said Rosie.

"Well, you can't." Tiffany threw me into her open handbag. "You can have her when we get back," she said. "That little doll has caused enough trouble already."

Tiff quickly zipped up her handbag and I was plunged into darkness.

CHAPTER 5

Tiffany's bag rocked from side to side like a rowing boat in a storm as she walked along.

Just when I thought I might be seasick, the swaying stopped. We must be at Rosie's house. There was a heavy *THUMP* as Tiffany threw her handbag down.

Above me the zip opened and Rosie pulled me out by my head.

"Come on, Princess Tiny-Twinkle. Time for your makeover," she said.

Peering through Rosie's fingers, I caught a

glimpse of Tiffany lying back on a SQUASHY white sofa in the lounge. She was already reading her magazine again.

Rosie danced out of the room, still clutching me tightly in her hand.

Her house was enormous. There were marble pillars, big gold banisters and a shiny glass chandelier hanging in the hall. . . All these shot by as Rosie galloped up the stairs.

Her bedroom was HUGE too. I felt as if I was in a giant toyshop. Everywhere I looked, there were dolls. They were on the bed and on shelves, on chairs and tumbling out of boxes. There were zillions of different kinds – rag dolls, fashion dolls, baby dolls, a set of Russian dolls jumbled up with their heads and bottoms all over the floor. . . There were doll cradles, doll clothes, doll bikes and an enormous doll's house with a red front door.

I wouldn't mind living in there, I thought. *Everything would be just the right size for me.*

But Rosie had other ideas. She laid me on her pink, fluffy carpet, lifted my leg in the air and pulled off my tiny shoe. *What was she doing?*

As soon as she let go, I wanted to drop my leg back down to the floor. But I remembered I was supposed to be a doll, so my leg wouldn't flop down. I kept it stuck in the air.

Rosie pulled the other leg up. She took off my other shoe. Then she leant over and tugged at my shorts.

Eek. This was *so* embarrassing. Rosie was undressing me. Completely!

She tossed my beautiful CAMOUFLAGE shorts up on to her dressing table. They were still tiny, of course, because I had been wearing them when I shrank.

"We'll get rid of those yucky things," she said. "And your grubby T-shirt. It's all covered in chocolate."

Yikes! I was left in nothing but my vest and knickers.

I could feel my face burning.

I must be blushing as pink as Rosie's carpet, I thought.

I was sure she'd notice, but she crawled away to rummage through a basket of dolls' clothes.

"Time to find you something pretty and princessy to wear," she said.

"Too babyish!" she sighed, throwing a baby doll's romper suit to one side.

"Too schooly." She threw out a doll's summer uniform. It was blue-and-white check, exactly like the ones we wear at school.

"Too night-timey." A pair of doll's pyjamas followed.

"You're too small and tiny for these silly clothes anyway," pouted Rosie. She threw out piles of outfits for bigger dolls as she sorted through the basket with her back to me.

Time to escape. I jumped up.

My bare feet sank into the soft, pink carpet, as if I were walking through a candyfloss meadow.

As soon as I'm out of here, I thought, *I'll . . . oh no. . .* I stopped.

What was I thinking of? I couldn't leave. Not in my knickers! What if I suddenly grew back to **FULL SIZE** halfway down the stairs . . . or worse still, in the middle of the street? How would I explain that I'd decided to run around town in nothing but my vest and purple polka-dot pants? I'd have to wait for Rosie to find me some new clothes. I glanced helplessly at my shorts, out of reach on the edge of the dressing table.

"Goodie, this will fit," said Rosie. I just had time to flop flat on my back again with my legs in the air before she turned round. "It belongs to my *Patty Pocket* doll . . . but I lost her."

I've seen tiny *Patty Pocket* dolls in the shops.

They're exactly the same size as me when I'm shrunk. Easy to lose. She'd probably been dropped behind a radiator or under a chest of drawers somewhere.

"Here you are, Princess Tiny-Twinkle," said Rosie, pulling me up by my hair again. I *wished* she wouldn't do that. "You're going to look so pretty."

She was holding a small green rubber suit with a frilly silver fishtail hanging off the end.

"You're going to be a princess mermaid," she grinned.

CHAPTER 6

Rosie almost broke my arm as she bent it backwards SQUASHING and PULLING me into the tiny rubber mermaid suit.

At last the dress was on. I could barely breathe it was so TIGHT. It came right down past my ankles with my feet just poking out of the bottom and the tail dragging along behind.

Rosie bounded across the room away from me. "Now you're a princess mermaid, you need sparkles," she said, grabbing a tube of greeny-blue glitter glue out of a big box with

ART THINGS written on the side.

She smeared shimmering GOO all over me – even on my toes. There was nothing I could do except lie still. She swirled it over my cheeks and lips and prodded me in the eye, trying to use it as eyeshadow. My top lashes stuck to my bottom lashes, gluing one eye shut.

"Look, Tiny-Twinkle," said Rosie. She picked up a little hand mirror from her dressing table and held it above me as I lay on the floor. "You look beautiful."

Even with only one eye open, I could see that I did *not* look beautiful. The mermaid dress was as tight as slug skin and the glitter was stuck all over me in big gooey spots.

"I wonder if the mermaid hairdresser is at Mermaid Cove today," said Rosie. "Let's swim over there and see if she can cut your hair."

Uh oh! This did not sound good.

Rosie crawled across the floor, swooshing me up and down in the air and bending my knees to make it look as if I was swimming along.

"Hello, Mr Hairdresser," she said, plunging her hand into the art box and pulling out a pair of round-ended scissors.

A lethal weapon.

I was pleased my eye was still stuck shut as

Rosie jabbed the scissors towards me. She started to hack at my fringe. A ragged tuft of hair fell to the floor . . . and then another.

This is going to look terrible. Mum had told me yesterday that I needed a haircut. I don't think this was what she had in mind.

"Not sharp enough," said Rosie, throwing the scissors down. "Wait there, Princess Tiny-Twinkle. My mummy's got a really SHARP pair."

"You're too young to play with scissors," I muttered as Rosie charged out of the room. Where was Tiffany? Babysitters are supposed to look out for this sort of thing.

But this was a chance to *ESCAPE*. The minute Rosie disappeared down the corridor, I scrambled up. It wasn't easy trying to move quickly in the mermaid suit. Every time I took a step, I kept tripping over.

"Stupid tail," I groaned. But there was no time to figure out a way to climb up the dressing table and rescue my lovely Stella Lightfoot shorts.

I needed to get out of here ... and fast. I touched my fringe and felt the gap where great chunks of hair had been taken out of it. That was just with paper scissors. If Rosie came back with the sharp ones, I'd probably end up bald ... or blind ... or she'd cut off my ear by mistake.

I rubbed my eyelashes until they blinked open from the glitter glue. Then I quickly pulled my shoes back on, hitched the mermaid skirt above my knees, draped the tail over my arm and STUMBLED to the door.

I could see a grand staircase. There must have been fifteen or twenty steps – each one three times as TALL as I was. It would take me half a day to climb down them. The pale blue carpet spread ahead of me, like a waterfall cascading to the hall below.

A waterfall! Of course! It would take hours to climb down each step . . . but how about if I rode them like rapids?

I WADDLED back to Rosie's room and found what I was looking for.

I remembered the Russian dolls I'd seen when I first came in. The whole stack was lying muddled up on the floor, all unscrewed so their hollow bottoms were in one place and their heads in another. I grabbed the largest one's bottom and rolled it to the top of the stairs. Then I went back for the big red-and-yellow smiling head.

I clambered into the bottom half of the Russian doll. It was as if I was standing in a bucket. I leant over the side, heaved her head up over me and twisted it tight. Now everything was dark, but I knew what I needed to do.

In last week's episode of **EXPLORE GALORE!**, Stella Lightfoot shot down a Canadian waterfall safe inside a barrel. My Russian doll should work just the same way on the stairs.

I leant my shoulder sideways and toppled over. The minute the doll was on her side she began to roll. **Clomp!**

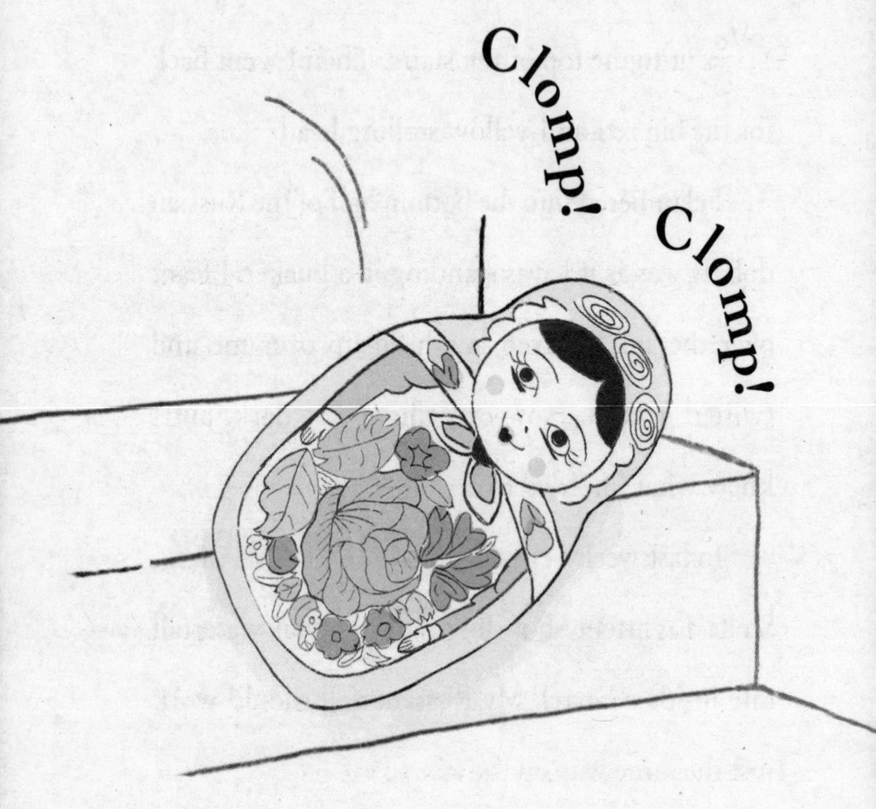

"Ouch," I yelped.

I'd forgotten water is soft and steps are hard – each thump on the stairs juddered my bones. Even so, it was utterly awesome . . . like a roller-coaster ride. I love roller coasters. They are the most exciting things in the whole world. The very first time I ever shrank I was about to ride a real one at a theme park.

"Yippee!" I cried, my voice echoing against the wood all around me. What was especially brilliant and scary about this ride was that I couldn't see where I was going. Everything was totally dark.

With one last BUMP, the doll stopped tumbling and began to roll smoothly along. I must have reached the marble floor of the hall.

BAM!

The doll crashed into something hard and popped open. I looked up and saw we had collided with a shoe rack.

I staggered to my feet, wishing I could have another go.

There was no time for that though. I had to get out of this house and find Nisha.

I tried to walk forward but I was too dizzy. I stumbled sideways and sank in a heap underneath the shoe rack.

"Yikes," I shivered. As my head stopped spinning, I noticed a pair of small dark eyes staring out at me from under the shoes.

"Who's that?" I whispered. "Who's there?"

I crawled slowly forward on my hands and knees, blinking as I peered into the gloomy world of dust and cobwebs under the shoe rack.

"Hello," I whispered, squinting at the figure in the shadows. "*Patty Pocket*? Is that you?"

Sure enough, Rosie's little lost doll was staring out at me. She was sitting inside a toy car. I **PUSHED** her gently towards the light to get a proper look. Her hair was long and blonde and **curly**. She was wearing a little bikini with pink dolphins on it. I thought about swapping clothes for a moment but decided it would be even more embarrassing to run around town in a bikini than in a mermaid suit.

"Pity," I shrugged. *Patty* really was exactly the same size as me. But it was her car that made me smile. She was sitting behind the steering wheel of a **BRIGHT PINK BEACH BUGGY**.

"Wow!" I grinned. As long as I stayed tiny, I could drive to the bookshop in that. I could find Nish.

I shut my eyes and tried to picture a map of town. We were somewhere near the top of Hill Street. And it's not called Hill Street for nothing – it slopes all the way down to the main road by the park. Perfect.

I SQUEEZED round the back of the beach buggy and pushed it towards the front door. If I could just get it out through the cat flap, I could escape.

"Sorry about this," I said, grabbing *Patty* around her middle and pulling her out of the driving seat.

"Humph!" It isn't easy lifting someone your own height, but I bent her at the waist and heaved her on to my shoulder in a fireman's lift. I've tried this with Nish a million times. At least *Patty* didn't wriggle – or scream – or say I was tickling her.

"There you go," I smiled as I plonked *Patty* on the doormat. I bent her waist and left her sitting as if she were sunbathing on the sand. Rosie would be sure to find her.

For now, I could still hear Rosie singing upstairs in her mum's bathroom. She must have forgotten all about me and my haircut.

"Good thing or I might be bald by now," I whispered, straightening *Patty's* curls.

I giggled to myself as I realized I was talking to a tiny plastic doll as if she were a real live friend.

"Got to go," I grinned. "Thanks for lending me the car. I'll get it back to you somehow..."

Suddenly, Rosie thundered to the top of the stairs.

"Tiffney!" she shouted. I grabbed the beach

buggy and pulled it into the shadows just in time.

I glanced up and gasped... Even from down here, I could see that Rosie's beautiful long blonde hair was now as short and bristly as a brush. She was holding her mum's sharp scissors in one hand and pile of golden curls in the other.

"Tiffney! T-I-F-F-N-E-Y!" she called, grinning from ear to ear. "I've cut my hair. Come and see!"

I peeped out from behind the beach buggy as Tiffany wandered in from the kitchen ... and SCREAMED.

"I'll call you back, Monique," she cried, dropping her mobile phone. "Rosie! What have you done? Your mum's going to kill me."

'Don't you like it?" Rosie burst into tears. "I practised on Princess Tiny-Twinkle first."

As Tiffany shot up the stairs, I rolled the beach buggy forward. In all the commotion, no one was looking my way. I pushed the little car from behind – like a supermarket trolley – bumping it through the cat flap.

As soon as I was outside, I SCRAMBLED into the seat behind the steering wheel. The sun was shining – not a cloud in the summer sky.

"The perfect day for a drive," I smiled, pulling on a pair of *Patty's* miniature sunglasses, which had been left on the seat.

"Looking good," I said, checking my reflection in the little tinfoil mirror. Now all I had to do was find Nisha. She must be worried sick by now. The last place she had seen me was in the park. I was sure she would go back there to look for me as soon as she knew I was lost.

If only we could be back together in time to see Stella Lightfoot, I thought, gripping the little steering wheel in my hands.

I had escaped from a terrible life of toy torture – no more haircuts or glitter – but this wasn't going to be easy. I stared at the wide tarmac driveway and listened to the **ROAR** of traffic on the busy road beyond. . .

CHAPTER 8

There was no floor in the toy beach buggy, so I was able to push the ground beneath me with the tips of my toes. The harder I pushed, the *FASTER* the car rolled forward.

Then . . . VROOM! I was away . . . steering wildly as the little buggy sped down the slope. It was like driving a runaway go-kart.

I SWERVED, heaving the steering wheel sharply to the left. I'd be safe if I kept well away from the road. There was no need to go anywhere near the traffic. I stayed tucked in close to the garden fences along the back of the pavement. I wouldn't get run over up here and no one would see me either as I WHIZZED along in the cool shadows.

I passed a mum with a pushchair who didn't even glance in my direction.

"What a ride," I cried as I hurtled down the hill. A breeze was blowing in my hair.

I skidded round a pothole and steered perfectly between a sharp stone and a mound of sticky chewing gum. This was even better than the dodgems at the fair. I've always said I'd be a great driver. But Dad never lets me have a go in our car. Not even when I begged him at a completely empty campsite once.

I gripped the little pink steering wheel. It was amazing, racing along twice as fast as I could have walked. In no time at all, I was rolling alongside the busy main road opposite the park.

"Hmm." I peered out from under my sunglasses. I was safe on the pavement for now. But at some point, I'd have to find a way to cross the road to reach the park. Nisha was most likely to be in the sandpit, searching where she'd last seen me.

If I waited by the pedestrian lights, someone would be sure to spot me. Some new little girl might snatch the beach buggy and take me home for more home-made beauty treatments.

"Poor Rosie," I murmured, as I remembered how proud of herself she'd looked when she appeared at the top of the stairs. Her hair was so short there was nothing left but tiny spikes like a . . . *hang on a second. . .*

"Like a *hedgehog*," I gasped. I had a brilliant plan.

I pushed my feet along the ground as fast as I could. The council had built a special mini underpass so that hedgehogs from the park could cross the busy main road safely without being SQUISHED. If I went through there, I could get to the other side without being seen . . . and without being SQUASHED myself.

It was our class at school who had started a petition asking the council to build the Hedgehog Underpass in the first place. We gathered hundreds of signatures saying that it wasn't fair the poor little hedgehogs kept being run over. We helped raise money for the tunnel. I'd even written to Stella Lightfoot, asking if she would come and cut the ribbon at the opening ceremony. She never wrote back. Mum said I couldn't expect her to – a superstar celebrity like Stella Lightfoot is far too busy.

VROOM! I whizzed on down the side of the pavement. Two minutes and I'd be at the tunnel.

I took my hands off the steering wheel and

raised them in the air for a second, as if I was riding a roller coaster.

"Whee!" I sped around a sharp bend in the pavement.

But the buggy suddenly hit a BUMP.

"Ahhhhh," I yelled as I flew through the air. My sunglasses spun off my nose and. . .

"Uh oh!" I felt my tummy turn a somersault. Even in mid-air, I knew this feeling. It was as if fireworks were exploding inside me. I was shooting back to **FULL SIZE**.

A second later, I was skidding along the ground fully grown.

"Look out!" A cyclist swerved sideways on the pavement, narrowly missing me as she sped around the corner. *Patty's* funky sunglasses were

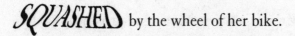

SQUASHED by the wheel of her bike.

I flung out my hand and grabbed the tiny pink beach buggy before she *skidded* on it.

"Sorry," she squealed.

Mum is always shouting at grown-up cyclists when they ride on the pavement. But this one didn't need telling off. She already looked as white as a sheet.

"Are you all right?" she said, screeching to a stop and pushing back her helmet. "I didn't see you. It was like you came out of nowhere."

"Yes. . . I. . . Er. . . Well. . ." I sat in a heap and looked down at my hands. There was a graze on my palm but nothing worse than that. "I'm fine," I smiled.

Poor woman. She looked really shaken up. But how could I explain that she couldn't have seen me – just a moment before I'd been the size of a key ring.

"You must be on the way to a fancy-dress

party," she smiled as she helped me stand up.

I had completely forgotten I was still wearing the rubber mermaid suit.

"I'm going to find my best friend," I said as the lady led me safely to the pedestrian crossing (there was no point in trying to fit through the hedgehog pass now). "We're off to the bookshop together," I said, hopping across the road with my mermaid tail tucked over my arm. "We're going to meet Stella Lightfoot. Just as long as she's still there. . ."

I hurried across the park as fast as I could. I soon found that BOUNCING on two feet like a bunny rabbit was much easier than trying to walk in the mermaid suit. I ignored all the funny looks I was getting, leaping out of the way just in time when a dog tried to bite my tail.

Boing boing boing! I sprang along.

Everything was going to work out fine. I had escaped from Rosie. I was back to full size. All I had to do now was find Nisha.

I headed straight across the grass towards the

playground and **UDDERLY PERFECT**.

But the minute I came bouncing round the side of the community centre, I could see that something was wrong.

Yellow-and-black stripy tape was crossed over the doorway of the café like a police crime scene. A sign had been nailed up saying:

DANGER!
KEEP OUT!
CLOSED UNTIL FURTHER NOTICE!

The skinny man in the white coat was standing on the doorstep frowning like a thundercloud. He was balanced on one foot, clutching his clipboard and dangling the other foot in mid-air. He had one of Mo's brooms turned upside down under his armpit like a crutch.

Oh dear! I remembered how Nisha and I had

heard him fall. I'd thought he was all right but he must have twisted his ankle or something.

"Health and safety is a very important issue, madam," he was saying, shaking his finger at Mo. "A community café like this is a place for children and young families. We cannot afford to take any risks. At the first sign of danger we have to close you down."

"Danger?" sighed Mo. "It was one spilt milkshake."

I could see from a gold badge pinned neatly to his pocket that the man's real name was Mr O. Zeal. The badge also said that he was a RISK EVALUATION OFFICER from Swanchester Town Council, Health and Safety Department. Mo was in big trouble . . . and all because of me.

I felt a crimson blush burning underneath the smudges of green mermaid glitter left on my face.

"Sir." I bunny-bounced forward and tugged Mr White Coat's sleeve.

"Please, Mr Zeal, sir . . . it's my fault you slipped on the milkshake," I explained, tugging his sleeve again. "I spilt it. I should have cleaned it up, but I was in a hurry and. . ."

"*You* should have cleaned it up?" Mr Zeal scratched his bristly moustache as if he was confused. "Do you work at the UDDERLY PERFECT Café?"

"N-no," I stuttered. "Not really. I do jobs for Mo sometimes, but. . ."

"Jobs?" Mr Zeal stared at me. "Do you get paid for this work, young lady?"

"Of course not." I shook my head. I had a horrible feeling I had said something wrong. Mo was LOOKING UP towards the sky, not making eye contact with me.

"Sometimes I get free milkshakes or doughnuts – that's all," I explained.

"I see." Mr Zeal clicked the end of his thin silver biro. He wrote something carefully on his clipboard, then he hobbled towards his white van, which was parked neatly in the delivery bay.

"This café will remain **CLOSED UNTIL FURTHER NOTICE**," he said.

"But you can't close down the café." I hopped after him. "What about all Mo's customers? Everyone LOVES her milkshakes . . . they're the **BEST** in the world. Did you try one?"

"No. I did not." Mr Zeal leant against the side of his van and handed Mo back her broom.

"You won't get away with this," she said. "I'll lodge a formal complaint."

"Please do. But the HEALTH AND SAFETY DEPARTMENT will agree with my findings," said Mr Zeal. "First there is the dangerous spillage of slippery liquid – which in this event caused personal injury to a council employee." He pointed towards his ankle. "And now I have uncovered additional evidence of unpaid child labour."

"That is simply not true," said Mo. "I don't have any children working here."

Mr Zeal poked a bony finger at me. "This young. . ." He looked confused for a moment as if he didn't know quite how to describe me. "This

the multi-storey car park."

"Well, I'm not beaten that easily," said Mo. She frowned at her mobile phone. "It doesn't look like anybody is going to answer. I'll have to go down to the town hall myself."

"Wait, Mo," I said as she picked up her handbag. "I'm . . . I'm really sorry. You wouldn't even be in this mess if it wasn't for me."

"Rubbish." Mo took hold of my face in both hands. "You look at me, Violet Potts. This is not your fault. This is silly grown-ups making silly rules, that's all. Do you understand me?"

I nodded. Mo doesn't stand for any nonsense from anybody. No matter how bad something seems, she can always make it better.

She raised an eyebrow. "Why exactly *are* you

dressed as a mermaid, Violet?" She squinted at me. "And who has been cutting your hair?"

"It's a long story," I said, smoothing down my fringe. I realized I was still holding the little beach buggy too.

"Well, don't stand here feeling sorry for yourself," said Mo. "If you really want to help me, you can talk to your friends. Start a petition – Save UDDERLY PERFECT From Being Closed Down. Get everyone we know to sign it."

"A petition?" I said, hitching up my mermaid skirt. "That's it . . . I've had an idea. A fantastic idea. UDDERLY PERFECT really can be saved."

I hopped away across the sandpit as fast as I could go.

"Hedgehogs," I called over my shoulder. "You'll see. Leave it all to me."

My plan was totally tremendous. If a petition had saved the hedgehogs from being SQUASHED, we could save the café in the same way. But if the idea was going to work, I had to see Stella Lightfoot and convince her to join our campaign. The local papers would write all about it if a real CELEBRITY was involved. It would be on the news and everything. The council would have to listen to us then.

First, I needed to find Nisha.

As I hopped across the sandpit, I nearly tripped over her. She was CROUCHING DOWN, combing through the sand with a little plastic fork.

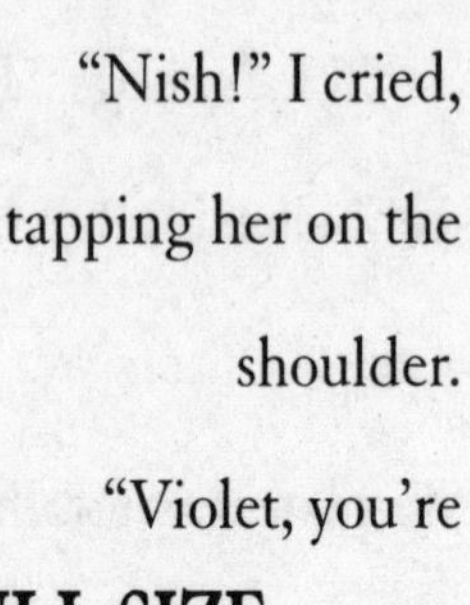

"Nish!" I cried, tapping her on the shoulder.

"Violet, you're **FULL SIZE**. You're safe!" Nish threw her arms around my neck. "I didn't realize you had fallen out of my pocket until I got all the way to the bookshop," she said. "I searched everywhere in case I'd dropped you on the high street. Then I came back here. I thought you were still TINY." Nish waved the plastic fork in the air. "That's why I'm using this." She scraped it across the sand as if to demonstrate. "I thought you were—"

"...buried in the sandpit like a miniature Egyptian mummy?" I took the fork and tossed it into the litter bin. "I very nearly was. But listen, Nish, we've got to go. We need to head back to town and catch Stella Lightfoot if we still can."

"I think she'll be gone already," said Nisha. "And surely you don't want to meet her dressed up like that." Nish tried not to laugh as she pointed at my green mermaid suit.

"I thought you *liked* mermaids," I said. "You're always pretending to be one when we go swimming."

"I do like mermaids," giggled Nish. "But it looks like one of the sharks that *you* always pretend to be has taken a bite out of your fringe. And where are your new shorts? You mum will go mad if you've lost them."

"Still shrunk," I groaned. "I had to leave them behind. At least *Patty* might get to wear them. They should be her size."

"Who's *Patty*?" asked Nish. "And why are you carrying that little pink car?"

"I'll explain everything on the way to the bookshop," I said. "Come on!"

I grabbed Nisha's hand. If we were going to see Stella Lightfoot, we didn't have a moment to lose.

Behind me, someone tugged on my tail.

"Are you a weal mermaid?" said a small voice.

I spun round and saw that the dribbly boy was still playing in the sandpit.

"Totally real," I grinned, waving my tail. "I'm a friend of Rosie's."

The little boy's eyes were as **wide** as fishcakes.

"Weally? But I know Wosie," he said.

"Good. You can give her this next time you see her," I said, holding out the little beach buggy. "Say Princess Tiny-Twinkle sent it."

With that, Nisha and I hurried away.

As we headed out of the park, I explained everything that had happened with Rosie and how I had become her doll. Then I told Nisha about the trouble our spilt milkshake had caused for Mo.

"That's why we have to get Stella Lightfoot to help us," I said.

"But she never even wrote back to you about the hedgehog petition," said Nisha.

"Only because she's too busy to read letters. Think about it," I said. "She's usually in the jungle. Or up a mountain. I bet thousands of fans write to her every day. But if we see her now – in person – at the bookshop, we can explain how important it is. She'll definitely help us. I know she will."

I pulled Nish down the street, hopping along as fast as I could.

"You know what Stella says at the end of every episode of EXPLORE GALORE!," I reminded her.

"Dare to dream – make your dreams happen, whatever your dreams may be!" we both chorused.

"UDDERLY PERFECT is Mo's dream," I said. "She worked really hard and saved up for years to make it happen. We can't let her lose it now . . . not when the spilt milkshake was all our fault. Even it was an accident. . ."

"Look!" cried Nisha, pointing down the street. We could see Pages Bookshop at last. A long white limousine pulled up outside it.

"I bet that's come to collect Stella," I said. "Come on, Nisha. Run!"

"Hello!" I shouted, calling out to the limousine driver. The long white car was parked up against the pavement like an enormous whale.

"Are you here for Stella Lightfoot?" I asked, *STUMBLING* forward with Nisha. There was a sticker in the back window saying Swanchester Limousines: Available For Private Hire.

"Might be," sniffed the driver, straightening his shiny black cap. He spat on a cloth and rubbed at an invisible smudge on the already gleaming bonnet. "I'm afraid I am not at liberty to say."

But just at that moment, the door to Pages Bookshop swung open and a crowd of people spilt on to the street.

"Wow!" I grabbed hold of Nisha's hand as Stella Lightfoot – *the* actual REAL-LIFE Stella Lightfoot – stepped out on to the pavement just a few metres away from us.

"Stamp on my toe, Nish," I hissed. "Stamp on it quick before I shrink with excitement."

"Really?" said Nish, looking worried. But before I could answer, she stamped . . . **HARD**.

"Yow!" I let out a scream of pain. Stella Lightfoot glanced in my direction, her long blonde ponytail swishing in the air as she turned her head.

"She's so pretty," whispered Nish.

Stella was wearing her famous purple and black CAMOUFLAGE shorts and a T-shirt with a picture of an open-mouthed shark saying:

She had nothing on her feet except thin green flip-flops. She might only have been standing on Swanchester High Street but, in my head, I could see her looking just the same if she was marooned on a desert island or canoeing down the Amazon.

"Wow!" I gasped again. She just looked so . . . so *shiny*. And ADVENTUROUS.

"It's funny to think of Stella in a limousine, isn't it?" I said to Nish as we pushed our way through the crowd that was now blocking the pavement. "On telly, she's always in a hot-air balloon. Or a helicopter . . . or riding an elephant."

"Where's she going to get an elephant in Swanchester?" laughed Nish as I tried to SQUEEZE past a lady with a buggy.

Stella was almost at the car.

"Wait," I shouted. "Miss Lightfoot!" I was surprised how **loud** my voice came out, but the driver had already opened the limousine door. I had to get Stella's attention. I had to stop her before she drove away and vanished for ever.

"Stella! I need your help," I cried. Nisha's hand slipped from my fingers as the woman with the buggy pushed between us. Stella turned her head.

A little smile flickered across her face. I wished I wasn't meeting my all-time hero dressed in a fishy mermaid suit – but at least I had her attention.

"It's my friend Mo," I said, waddling forward. "She runs a café." My heart was beating so fast it felt as if a herd of buffalo were stampeding inside my chest. Out of the corner of my eye, I could see a man with a television camera making his way through the crowd.

"A café? That's nice," Stella Lightfoot smiled, but she was already turning away again.

"It – it's like you always say on your show, about … about dreams," I stuttered. My voice wasn't loud and clear any more. It had gone all SQUEAKY and HIGH. But I had to make Stella understand. I waved my hands, smiling at Nisha and hoping she would join in.

"*Dare to dream*," we both said. But it wasn't just Nisha who helped me out.

"*. . .make your dreams happen, whatever your dreams may be!*" chorused the whole crowd together.

"Gosh," Stella smiled. "I see I've got a lot of **EXPLORE GALORE!** fans here." There was a flash of tiny lights like fireworks as everybody held up cameras or mobile phones and snapped a picture.

"What's your name, Little Miss Mermaid?" Stella asked.

The crowd laughed.

"I'm Violet," I said. "I – I don't even like mermaids. Not really. I'm more of a . . . of an adventure kind of person." I pointed helplessly at Stella's T-shirt. "I love sharks. They're amazing."

"Well, Violet," said Stella. "If you like adventure, I guess you must be a pretty big fan of my show?"

"**EXPLORE GALORE!**." I gulped and the crowd cheered. "I completely and utterly, absolutely, totally love it."

"Tell you what then," winked Stella. "I'll sign your tail."

Before I even realized what was happening, she clicked her fingers. A woman in a baseball cap with a long blonde ponytail just like Stella's handed her a thick black felt-tip pen.

"There you are, Stella," the woman mumbled from underneath her cap. It was almost as if she was trying to hide her face. She was also wearing dark glasses – although maybe that was just because it was such a sunny day.

"Thanks," said Stella, bending down. She pulled the lid off the pen with her teeth and scribbled her name across the bottom of my rubber tail.

S. Lightfoot x

"Don't let the sharks nibble that, Little Mermaid," she joked, turning back towards the car.

"Wait!" I cried. "I haven't told you about Mo and her café. I haven't explained why we need your help—"

"Send me a letter." Stella tossed the felt-tip pen back to the woman with the ponytail and dark glasses. "You'll find a fan mail address on my website."

She was already bending her knee to climb into the limousine.

"I have to go," she said, waving to the crowd as the driver stepped between us. "I'm going to find somewhere nearby to pitch my tent for the night. Then I'll head to the airport in the morning. I'm off on safari tomorrow."

"Good luck! Don't get eaten by a lion," called a lady standing near the bookshop. Everyone laughed and cheered. The man with the telly camera ran forward with a big hairy microphone (it looked a bit like my dog Chip).

"Cheerio," said Stella, smiling into the camera.

I grabbed at the open limo door.

"But I wrote to you once before," I said. "About hedgehogs. You didn't reply."

"Hedgehogs?" Stella smiled. "I love hedgehogs. Your letter must have got lost. Write to me again. I want to hear all about your prickly problem." She laughed with a tinkling sound like a teaspoon hitting a glass.

"But this isn't about hedgehogs. Not this time," I said as Stella stepped into the limousine and it swallowed her up. "It's about Mo. You have to listen," I begged as the car started. "I need your help. We have to save UDDERLY PERFECT."

My words were lost in the roar of the engine as the limousine pulled away.

"*Dare to dream!*" cried Stella from the open window.

The crowd cheered.

She was gone.

As soon as Nisha's mum dropped me home, I sped past Dad in the doorway and scrambled upstairs to change out of my mermaid suit before Mum could ask any questions about where I had left my new CAMOUFLAGE shorts.

Then I spread my felt-tip pens on the coffee table and started to make a **Save Udderly Perfect** poster. My meeting with Stella Lightfoot had not gone at all as I had hoped. But I refused to give up. Even if I had to march round town in an inflatable cow suit handing out leaflets to keep the café open, I would.

Nisha and I had agreed we'd both make a poster. Hers would be amazing, of course, because she's really artistic. My drawing of a cow looked more like a spotty hippopotamus. I just was wondering whether adding a big pink udder would help, when Dad leapt off the sofa.

"Violet, look!"

I almost jumped out of my skin.

"It's you," he cried, waving the TV remote in the air. "You're on the local news."

He clicked the telly on to pause. The picture was FROZEN . . . and there I was, standing in the middle of the screen right next to Stella Lightfoot. I was dressed as a giant mermaid, of course.

"Josie, come and see. You're not going to

believe this," hollered Dad, calling Mum through from the kitchen.

"Gracious," gulped Mum, seeing me on the screen.

"This is *so* embarrassing!" flushed Tiff, who was back from babysitting. "What if any of my friends see you?"

"Shh!" said Dad. "I'll rewind it and we can record as we view." Dad is CRAZY about gadgets and it was hard to tell if he was more excited that his youngest daughter was on the news or that he got to show off the wonders of his new SUPER-SMART TV.

"Spot on!" he whooped, throwing his arms in the air as if he were a footballer scoring a goal. All he had done really was rewind the news to the exact point when they started talking about me.

"*And finally*," smiled the reporter in the studio, "*we'll leave you with pictures of the celebrity adventurer – the star of* **EXPLORE GALORE!** *– Stella Lightfoot, on a visit to Swanchester earlier today. . .*"

They cut to a picture of the high street. There I was, standing beside the limousine. The man with the television camera must have filmed us. You could see Stella Lightfoot taking the pen from the secretive-looking woman with the ponytail and dark glasses. Then she walked towards me, signed my tail and smiled her famous Stella Lightfoot smile.

"That's one local girl who certainly made a

SPLASH!" chuckled the newsreader. "Now for the weather. . ."

That was it. Half a second of me dressed as a mermaid and it was over. If only the cameraman had interviewed me – I could have told him about the campaign to save Mo's cafe. That was exactly the sort of publicity we needed.

Even so, I couldn't help smiling . . . I had got to meet Stella Lightfoot in actual real life. *And* she had signed my mermaid tail. I'd write to her tomorrow and beg her to help us. Perhaps I could even call the news station and tell them all about **UDDERLY PERFECT** myself.

"I am totally, totally ***FAMOUS***," I grinned.

"Yes. For being dressed like a fish," sighed

Tiff. She had been in a foul mood ever since she'd got home. Probably because Rosie's mum had given her the sack. She'd exploded – *like a bomb*, Tiff told us – saying she was a terrible babysitter for not noticing that Rosie was cutting her hair.

Tiff sank into an armchair, turning her back on the TV.

"I can't believe it," chuckled Dad, rewinding and **FREEZING** again on the picture of me and Stella.

"What I can't believe is why Violet's dressed up in that strange costume," said Mum, pointing at the screen. "What happened to your new CAMOUFLAGE shorts? The pair you pestered me to buy because Stella Lightfoot wears the same ones?"

Mum turned and folded her arms. "And what possessed you to cut your hair?" she asked. "At least Rosie has an excuse. She's only little. What have you got to say for yourself?"

"Erm. . ."

BRING! BRING! Like a fire engine coming to the rescue of a burning building, I heard the phone ringing in the hall.

"Don't think I've finished with you, young lady," Mum warned as she ran to answer it.

"Great," I mumbled under my breath. Today had been a total disaster. I had managed to lose a brand-new pair of shorts, have a really bad haircut and close down Mo's café. That was a record, even for me.

I have to find a way to put things right, I thought,

leaning forward and staring at the picture of Stella Lightfoot frozen on the TV.

While Mum was talking on the phone in the hall, Tiffany's mobile started to beep too.

"This is so embarrassing," she moaned, reading her texts. "*Everyone* has seen you on telly."

"I didn't know your friends watched the news – I thought they were too busy checking their lipstick," I giggled, peering over her shoulder.

Ur little sis so cute ♥, said one message.

V adorable ☺, said a text from Monique.

Gr8 mermaid suit.

Meeting Stella L! Respect!

"See. Told you I was totally famous," I smiled, punching Tiff on the arm.

Mum came back into the room. She was smiling too, as if she had forgotten about the lost shorts – at least for the moment. "That was Gran – she was calling on her new mobile phone, can you believe it?"

"Gran with a mobile," snorted Tiffany. "That's hilarious."

"Her number is easy to remember," said Mum. "It's just 077, then your birthday, Tiffany, followed by Violet's."

"What make of phone did she get?" asked Dad.

"I don't know. I didn't ask," said Mum, raising her eyebrows. "Everyone at the Sunset Retirement Centre saw you on telly, Violet. Gran says to tell you Cora and Dora, Mr Gupta and Nurse Bridget all thought you were totally AWESOME . . . although I'm sure that's not actually the word they used."

"I bet it *was*," I said. I love the old people at the retirement centre where Gran lives. Ever since I helped solve a string of mysterious robberies that happened there (that was my first ever real shrinking adventure) they always say I'm their ABSOLUTE FAVOURITE visitor.

"I've asked Gran to come over and look after you tomorrow," said Mum.

"Now that really is *awesome*," I grinned. I could get Gran help me write a letter to Stella. She could sign the petition to save UDDERLY PERFECT. She'd get all the other old people involved too.

"She's going to watch you while I'm at work,"

said Mum. "I'm not sure I trust Tiffany to babysit after what happened with Rosie."

"I'm meeting Monique anyway," huffed Tiff.

"Gran says she's looking forward to a mini adventure or two," said Mum, shrugging her shoulders. "I don't know what she meant by that."

"Good old Gran," I said. I knew at once she was thinking about shrinking. She's the only one who really knows how exciting it can be.

"Whatever else you get up to, I've told Gran she has to take you into town to get a proper haircut," sniffed Mum.

CHAPTER 13

Next morning Gran arrived clutching the local paper.

TAIL OF THE LITTLE MERMAID,

said the headline. Swanchester Girl Makes Waves.

"Great outfit!" chuckled Gran, waving the picture under my nose and pointing to my tail. "I'm disappointed you're not wearing it today. We could have gone for a swim."

"Very funny," I said as I led Gran through to the kitchen.

I was actually wearing a purple polka-dot frock which Mum had laid out for me this morning. Since I had lost my shorts, I wasn't going to argue with what she wanted me to wear.

Gran was dressed in a pair of sequined sparkly trousers and a T-shirt with a bright orange starfish on the front.

"You look a bit like a mermaid yourself," I teased. Gran always wears bright, crazy outfits that make me want to smile. She had a big stripy handbag too.

She opened it on the kitchen table and pulled out a packet of her favourite pink wafer biscuits . . . then two bottles of strawberry milkshake and some straws.

Mum and Dad had already left for work and Tiffany had just gone to meet Monique, so now we had the house to ourselves.

"Don't tell your mum I brought naughty treats. She wouldn't approve," winked Gran. "I know these milkshakes aren't as good as the ones Mo makes, but the colour matches the pink biscuits perfectly, don't you think?"

"Oh, Gran," I said. "Haven't you heard? **UDDERLY PERFECT** has been closed down . . .

by a health and safety inspector. They're going to take away Mo's licence."

"I read something about that in the paper," said Gran, squinting at the front page. "But I thought it must be a mistake. You know how the newspapers love to exaggerate and make things up."

Gran rummaged in her handbag and pulled out a shiny gold glasses case. She slipped a pair of small round spectacles on to the end of her nose. "There we are," she said, pointing to an article just below the picture of me and Stella Lightfoot.

***MO* FUTURE FOR DANGEROUS CAFÉ**, it said. **UDDERLY PERFECT CLOSED AFTER SHAMEFUL SLIP!**

"It says something about knocking the café

down and building a multi-storey car park," said Gran, running her finger down the page. "They're going to start work by the end of the month. That's outrageous."

"And so soon," I groaned. "They can't do that, can they?" I told Gran all about what had happened with Mr Zeal, the horrible inspector.

"Oh dear," said Gran. "All because you tipped over a milkshake when you shrank?"

"Exactly," I sighed. "So I have to do something to help."

"Hmm," said Gran, taking off her glasses and chewing the end of them thoughtfully. "I still don't understand how you wound up dressed as a mermaid?"

I explained how I had fallen out of Nisha's

pocket and become Rosie's toy princess.

Gran laughed so much that tears rolled down her cheeks.

But she cheered up when I told her how I'd thundered down the stairs inside the Russian doll. "Magnificent! No one else in the whole world has ever had a ride like it. Think of that."

I'd just got to the part about driving the mini beach buggy when the doorbell rang.

"Run and answer that," said Gran. "It'll be the taxi. I ordered one to take us to the hairdresser."

"No problem," I said. It was another hot day and as I opened the door, I squinted into the sunshine. It wasn't a taxi waiting outside . . . it was a long white LIMOUSINE.

I stared at the limousine parked in front of our house (at least, its bonnet was parked in front of our house . . . the rest of the car was so long, it was parked in front of next door too).

"Good morning, miss," said the driver. It was the same man who had driven the limo for Stella Lightfoot yesterday. He scuttled over to the side of the car and opened the door as if he was expecting someone to step in ... or *out*!

Stella Lightfoot, I thought. My heart was pounding as sunlight bounced off the dark windows. But it couldn't be. Why would Stella Lightfoot be coming to visit *me*?

Unless. . . My heart was thumping so hard now I was scared I would shrink from excitement. *Unless* she had seen the picture of us together on the news. Now she wanted to find out more about what I'd been saying . . . about the hedgehogs, perhaps?

"Hum," the driver coughed sharply. He was still holding the door. "Aren't you going to get in?"

"Me? Get in?" I peered into the dark limo. "But – but . . . I don't understand?"

"**SURPRISE!**" cried Gran. She bustled

on to the doorstep beside me, clutching her stripy bag. "I told you I'd ordered a taxi."

"'But this isn't a taxi," I said. "It's a—"

"A limousine. I know. Isn't it wonderful?" Gran's eyes twinkled. "I got the idea when I saw Stella Lightfoot driving away at the end of the newsflash. I called Swanchester Limos and hired one for us. I thought it would be fun. You're famous now you've been on telly, Violet. You have to travel in style." Gran clapped her hands.

"You mean, you asked for a limousine just to take us to the hairdresser?" I stammered, struggling to make sense of everything. The limo was empty. The driver wasn't bringing Stella Lightfoot here – he was collecting me ... as a treat. This was CRAZY – even for Gran.

"It's so totally glamorous!" I said, throwing my arms around her neck.

"Hum." The driver cleared his throat louder than ever. "I'm afraid we do need to get going. I have a very important client after you."

CHAPTER 14

As Gran and I **SPED** through town in the long white limousine, I imagined I was as famous as Stella Lightfoot. It even helped take my mind off Mo and the café for a while.

Gran poured us each a lemonade from the minibar. She held out her new mobile phone and took a picture of us clinking our **bubbling** glasses as if they were champagne.

"It's not just your dad who's good with technology," she chuckled.

Gran showed me the photo. She had completely

cut off the top of our heads. But it didn't matter. You could still see we were **GRINNING** from ear to ear.

"I think I need my specs," said Gran, peering at the screen.

"I'll get them," I said.

Gran's handbag was lying on its side and I could see that her gold glasses case had slid along the floor of the limo.

"Here," I said, CRAWLING FORWARD and passing it up to her.

"It's empty," groaned Gran. "I must have left my specs on your kitchen table when I was reading the newspaper."

"Hold on," I said. "There's something else here."

I pulled on the corner of a little zip-up bag poking out from under the minibar. My hands were shaking as I held it up.

"That's not mine," said Gran. "Looks like a make-up bag."

"But it's purple-and-black CAMOUFLAGE," I cried, rattling the bag under Gran's nose.

"I can see what colour it is, Violet," Gran laughed. "My eyesight may be bad but I'm not blind yet!"

"You don't understand," I said, bouncing on the seat. "This is Stella Lightfoot's. I am sure of it. All her clothes are purple-and-black CAMOUFLAGE. I bet she dropped the bag when she was in the limo yesterday."

I tugged at the BULGING zip. "I'll have a look inside."

"I'm not sure you should," Gran frowned. "It might be private."

But it was too late. I'd opened it already.

"Go on then. Just a quick peep," said Gran. "There might be something with a name on it. Though I expect it is only make-up."

I could see at once that Gran was wrong. There was one tube of lipstick and a little mirror – but no other make-up at all.

"It's weird. Everything else seems to be for cooking," I said, showing her a stack of mini cupcake cases. There were three pots of sprinkles, a little set of those different size measuring spoons and a small bottle of vanilla flavouring like the stuff Mo adds to her sponge cakes. There was also a biscuit cutter in the shape of a shark. Even though Stella's name wasn't on anything, I was more certain than ever that this was her bag.

"You know how much she loves sharks. Just like me," I said.

"Whoever it belongs to, they're certainly a keen cook," Gran said, taking a look for herself.

"There's a pack of crushed chilli peppers in here. And a jar of sea salt."

"Let's deliver the bag back to Stella in person," I said, clapping my hands. "I'll have a real reason to meet her again. I can tell her properly about Mo."

"I thought Stella was on safari?" said Gran.

"She said at the bookshop she wasn't going until this morning," I remembered, jiggling my feet in the air. "Perhaps she hasn't left for the airport yet. The limo driver must know where her campsite is. He dropped her there last night."

"Campsite? Why doesn't she stay in a hotel?" asked Gran, raising her eyebrows. "Surely she can afford it. . .?"

"Oh, Gran. She's Stella Lightfoot," I explained.

"She wouldn't stay in a hotel. She's WILD and BRAVE."

"All right. We'll ask the driver," said Gran. She leant forward to open the screen which cut off the driver from the rest of the limo.

"Steady though, Violet," she warned as I bounced along the seat opposite her. "Don't get overexcited. This would be a terrible time to shr—"

"Too late," I squeaked. My toes were TINGLING. My tummy POPPED – I was caught in mid-bounce as I flew up from the seat. By the time I landed, I had shrunk to the size of the lipstick in Stella Lightfoot's bag.

"Whoops," said Gran. But she had already hit the button to open the screen.

"Quick. Hide in here," she hissed, holding out her empty glasses case.

"Good plan, Gran." I leapt *forward* as the screen slid down.

But Gran's eyesight really must be getting bad.

SNAP!

She clicked the case shut. Too quick.

I was still flying through the air as the screen slid down.

I took a quick mid-air decision and threw myself sideways like an Olympic high-jumper.

PLOP!

I landed safely out of view in Stella's purple-and-black CAMOUFLAGE bag, which was still open on the seat.

"Hello. My name's Pete," the driver told Gran. "What can I do for you, madam?"

"We found this under the minibar," Gran explained. She held up the little bag to show him. She had no idea I had jumped inside, of course. "We think it might belong to Stella Lightfoot."

"I'll make sure she gets it back," said Pete, pulling over to the side of the road. As he took hold of the bag, I ducked under a measuring spoon.

"I'm actually due to collect Miss Lightfoot next," said Pete. "But . . . but wait a minute. What's going on?"

As he turned his head and looked properly into the back of the limo, his jaw dropped open with surprise. "Where has your granddaughter gone?"

As I peeped out through the open zip, I saw that Pete's eyes were as **wide** as headlamps.

"I don't understand," he said, swivelling round in his seat so he could see the whole limousine. "I saw her get in when I picked you up."

"Erm . . . Violet got out at the last set of traffic lights," said Gran quickly. "By the library. She . . . erm . . . she remembered she had a book to return."

I had a good view of Gran from inside the make-up bag. She was smiling happily, quite sure that I had landed safe inside her glasses case.

"I'll get out as well," she said. "There's no point in going to the hairdresser without Violet."

I could tell Gran wanted to escape from the limousine as quickly as possible – probably to open the glasses case so I could breathe. If I really were inside there I'd have been half suffocated by now.

She was holding it delicately on her lap as if it contained a rare butterfly.

"Psst! Gran. Over here." Even though Pete was still holding Stella's bag out in front of him, I risked poking my head up for a moment. I had to make Gran see me before she got out of the car.

But Pete's hand loomed towards me in its leather glove like a big black crow swooping down.

I ducked just in time as the zip slid closed over my head.

The bag swayed.

THUMP!

Everything clattered around me.

Pete must have thrown it down on the seat.

I heard doors open as he helped Gran out of the car.

"Cheerio," she called.

Her voice sounded far away already

"Goodbye, madam," said Pete.

The limo SHUDDERED as he turned on the engine.

A minute later, we were on the move. Gran was gone. I was on my own now.

It was dark and cramped inside the little bag. The shark fin on the biscuit cutter was digging into my back.

Stretching my foot, I managed to jiggle the zip open a bit and let in a stream of light.

Now that I could see what I was doing, I pushed my way up between the jars of sprinkles and peeped out of the gap.

Beside me, I could see that Pete, the limo driver had his eyes fixed on the road ahead.

Gran will be so worried when she realizes she has

lost me, I thought as we sped through town.

I had no idea how I would be able to find my way back to her again. Not even if I grew to **FULL SIZE**.

We'll have to drive right out to the countryside to find Stella Lightfoot's campsite, I thought.

But just five minutes later, we stopped. Pete climbed out of the car.

I stood on tiptoes, peeping out of the bag like a meerkat from its burrow.

Through the open window on the driver's side of the limo, I could see that we were outside a tall white marble building.

I read on a gold sign above a set of revolving doors. Why were we here? We were supposed to be picking up Stella Lightfoot. But this wasn't a campsite. It was the smartest hotel in Swanchester. Mum says some of the rooms have gold bathtubs and there's a really fancy restaurant with a world-famous French chef.

I could see Stella coming down the marble steps. She was wearing a purple-and-black CAMOUFLAGE jumpsuit with a jacket slung over her arm. She was also holding a purple-and-black CAMOUFLAGE suitcase. She must have stayed here overnight.

"Good morning, miss," said Pete, hurrying forward to take the case.

"You're late," snapped Stella.

As she reached the bottom of the steps, I could see her face clearly. She didn't say good morning to Pete or even smile at him. She just barged past, throwing her jacket on to the back seat of the limo and climbing in without another word.

I ducked down inside the camouflage bag, wishing I had found somewhere better to hide, as Pete scrambled back into the driving seat.

I can't believe I'm in the same car as Stella Lightfoot, I thought. *If only I could grow back to full size somehow when no one was looking. I'd be able to speak to her again. About Mo.*

"My last passengers found this, Miss Lightfoot," said Pete. He picked up the bag and it shot into the air so **FAST** my stomach lurched as if it had been left behind.

"Oh, I'm so happy to have this back," said Stella, as Pete passed the bag through the hatch. "I thought I'd lost it." She really did sound pleased.

From my hiding place under the jar of salt, I could see Stella through the open zip. She was smiling now – GRINNING from ear to ear. Her whole face lit up – just for a second. Then the smile was gone.

"Let's get moving," she growled, sounding all cross and grouchy again, just like Tiffany when I bounce on her bed in the mornings.

It was odd. I would never have thought of Stella as grumpy. She always seems so cheerful on television. But perhaps Pete really was very late.

"I better make myself look presentable," Stella sighed.

Before I knew what was happening, she grabbed the bag and turned it upside down. Everything came spilling out on to the seat beside her. Luckily, I was buried under the packet of crushed chilli peppers. Stella grabbed the little mirror from right next to me. As she flipped it open, I could see her looking at her own reflection.

I had to find somewhere to hide. And quickly.

CHAPTER 16

Holding a mini cupcake case above me like a crab in its shell, I *scurried* towards Stella's jacket, hoping to hide underneath it. But as I **SQUEEZED** between two pots of sprinkles on the seat, her hand shot d
o
w
n towards me.

"There should be a lipstick here somewhere," she muttered, still squinting into the mirror.

She brushed the cupcake case aside, and then her fingers closed around me. I **FROZE** – as still as a fish finger in a freezer compartment. I was terrified she would lift me up to her lips – after all, I was exactly the same size as the tube of lipstick.

Luckily, the car suddenly started to **BUMP** **from SIDE to SIDE**, shaking like a tambourine. It was as if we had left the main road and gone on to some sort of farm track.

"Are we nearly there?" said Stella, letting go of me and leaning forward to look out of the window.

"Nearly," said Pete.

I had no time to look out of the window myself. I spotted the real lipstick and kicked it towards Stella's leg. It rolled across the seat, bumping into her just as I dived under the nearby packet of chilli peppers.

Putting the lipstick on with one hand, Stella dug around in her jacket and pulled out a mobile phone.

"You'd better have everything ready," she barked, shouting at someone on the other end. "We'll be with you shortly."

As soon as the call was finished, she dropped the phone back into her jacket.

That pocket would make the perfect place to hide, I thought.

I **shot** *forward*.

ONE . . . TWO . . . THREE leaps and I was in.

I'd risked Stella seeing me. But it was worth it. I was well hidden now.

"Can't you drive any faster?" Through the open pocket, I could still hear Stella shouting at Pete. "I am supposed to be on safari, you know."

Of course. . . No wonder she was stressed. She was probably late for her plane. If she was going on safari, she must be flying to . . . to . . .

Jumping giraffes! I had to clamp my hand over my mouth to stop myself from shouting out. If Stella Lightfoot was going to Africa, I could go with her. All I'd need to do was stay hidden in her jacket.

I wanted to turn cartwheels and jump up and down. *I could go on an* **EXPLORE GALORE!** *EXPEDITION … WITH STELLA LIGHTFOOT … IN AFRICA.*

But, as soon as I thought it, I knew it was impossible. I couldn't fly away on safari. Not now. No matter how much I wanted to. Poor Gran had no idea where I was. Mum and Dad would be worried sick if they knew. I had to get back to Swanchester as quick as possible.

Most of all, I had to come up with a new plan

to save Mo's café. As I hadn't grown back to full size I couldn't ask Stella for help. I would have to do it without her.

Going on safari will have to wait, I thought. *I have important work to do.*

Stella's mobile phone was lying flat in the bottom of her pocket beside me. Typing with my feet like a TINY TAP DANCER, I quickly sent a message to Gran. I told her I was safe and promised I'd stay in the limo.

I remembered Gran's number was just 07, then Tiff's birthday followed by mine. I typed this in, then slid across the screen and pressed **SEND**.

I started to climb out of Stella's pocket again. I'd have to hide in the car until it went back to Swanchester after dropping her at the airport.

As soon as I was out in the light I clung to a button under a fold in the jacket. It wasn't easy to hold on. The car was still bumping wildly from side to side as it rattled down the uneven road.

Funny. We should be taking the motorway to reach the airport, I thought.

But a few moments later, the rocking stopped and we came to a halt.

"At last. We're here," said Stella.

I SLID TO THE FLOOR, ducking into the shadows just in time as she grabbed her jacket and stepped out of the limo.

I could see her waving her arms. She seemed to be shouting at a man with a film camera. Then they both disappeared from sight.

I crept forward and peered out of the open door. We were parked on a grassy track at the bottom of a very steep hill. Definitely *not* an airport. No plane could take off from here.

I strained my ears to see if I could hear voices. Stella and the cameraman were gone. Pete was nowhere to be seen.

Surely he'd be back in a minute. He must have left the door open by mistake.

I waited five minutes. Maybe ten. It seemed like hours.

There was nothing to look at except a lazy bumblebee **buzzing** around on the sunny hillside.

I knew I'd promised Gran I would stay in the limo, but it wasn't going back to Swanchester. Not yet. Not without Pete to drive it.

It can't do any harm to get out for a minute, I thought. *I'll just see what everyone is up to, then I'll hurry straight back.*

I turned around, dangling my legs out of the open door, and dropped on to the SOFT, SPRINGY grass below. I landed on my hands and knees like a squatting frog.

Before I'd even lifted my head, I noticed the smell. . . Something strong and musty and bitter – like a cat's litter tray that really, really needed changing.

"Poo!"

Perhaps being tiny made the stink twice as strong . . . but I was sure I recognized that pong from somewhere. What was it?

I wrinkled my nose and sniffed the air.

As I lifted my head, I knew what it was. The last time I had smelt that smell, I had been at the zoo.

I turned around very,

very

slowly

and looked behind me.

I was staring into the

WIDE OPEN *JAWS*

of an enormous crouching lion.

I FROZE for a moment – held in the lion's gaze. I stared up into his huge, dark orange eyes – like two setting suns above me.

I wanted to look away, but I couldn't. It was as if I was hypnotized. I could barely breathe. I know Stella Lightfoot said she was going on safari, but I thought she meant in Africa. I wasn't expecting wild animals here … wandering around. In England.

"Nice kitty," I whispered, my voice trembling as I spoke.

The lion's eyes flickered, watching me like a cat watches a mouse . . . except the lion was a zillion times **BIGGER** than any cat and I was still as SMALL as a mouse.

There was no sign of anyone else. Stella Lightfoot, Pete and the cameraman had completely disappeared. I wondered for one crazy moment if the lion had eaten them already – **CHOMP! CHOMP! CHOMP!** – a three-course meal. Now he'd finish off with me, like a tiny after-dinner mint.

No, I thought. I'd only seen them a little while ago. He couldn't' have gobbled them up yet. I remembered all the nature documentaries I have seen. Lions eat their prey slowly. . . They like to play with it first.

In front of me, the lion shifted his paws. Was he about to play with *me*?

I glanced out of the corner of my eye – not even daring to move my head. The limousine was still just behind me but there was no way I could scramble back inside.

"Good puss," I QUIVERED as a drip of sweat trickled off the end of my nose.

Although I was too small to climb into the car, perhaps I could roll underneath it, out of reach of the lion's claws.

Don't move fast, I told myself. I know what cats are like. Nisha and I help out at the PAW THINGS PET RESCUE CENTRE. Whenever we play with the kittens, they go crazy the minute something flashes past them. It doesn't matter if it's a feather on the end of a string or a fly on a windowpane – the moment it shifts, they pounce. I had a horrible feeling the lion would be the same . . . only bigger . . . and with much sharper claws.

One. . .

I bent my knees, very gently.

Two. . .

I slowly dropped my shoulders.

Thr—

BIFF!

Out of nowhere the lion's paw shot forward – too quick for me to see it coming. I was knocked to the ground.

BAM!

Now the lion had me, he was batting me

about from side to side.

Biff! From one paw.

Bam! Back to the other.

Each of the lion's paws was about the size of a table-tennis bat. I shot backwards and forwards across the short grass like a Ping-Pong ball.

BIFF!

At least his claws were tucked in. But every time he hit me, my breath was knocked out.

BAM! BIFF!

As long as he's playing, he's not ready to eat me, I thought. My head was ringing like the time I got kicked playing KungFu Warrior. *It's when he gets bored that I need to panic.*

"Whoa!"

The lion's huge paw came from above this time.

The game

was changing.

*FL*OMP!

He pinned me

down like a playing

card he was waiting

to turn over.

Staring up through the golden fur at the edge of the lion's paw, I saw him lift his other foot and lick it. As he cleaned between each toe, his claws shot out like knives – sharp steel knives, each one as long as I was.

Then the lion bent down and sniffed at my hair, his hot meaty BREATH almost choking me as I lay beneath his paw.

This is it, I thought, as a dribble of lion drool dropped on to my cheek. *He's going to eat me.* And the worst of it was, no one would ever know where I'd gone. One bite and he'd swallow me whole.

But instead, the lion lifted his head. His ears twitched.

"RORY! THERE YOU ARE, BOY!"

boomed a voice in the distance. "I've been looking everywhere for you."

A moment later the owner of the voice appeared, panting heavily beside us. He was an ENORMOUS red-faced man with a bristly moustache and a shaggy sandy-coloured beard. His eyebrows were just as bushy and he had a wild yellow mane of hair – all in all, he looked like a human lion.

Rory – the real lion – lifted his head and allowed it to be stroked.

I couldn't believe it. He was tame!

The man scratched him between his ears.

"Come on, Rory. Time you were doing some work," he said, slamming the limousine door. "What did you think you were going to do? Hop in there and go for a drive?"

He set off up the hill, calling to the lion.

Underneath Rory's paw I was still struggling to get out. But suddenly I felt him shift.

His huge shaggy head loomed down towards me. He caught the hem of my dress in his teeth and tossed me into the air.

He's going to open his jaws and swallow me like a peanut, I thought. My arms and legs were spinning wildly as I tried desperately to run away in mid-air.

"Help!" I squeaked.

But now, instead of Rory's snapping teeth, his broad golden back was beneath me. He wasn't going to eat me. He'd just thrown me in the air like a toy.

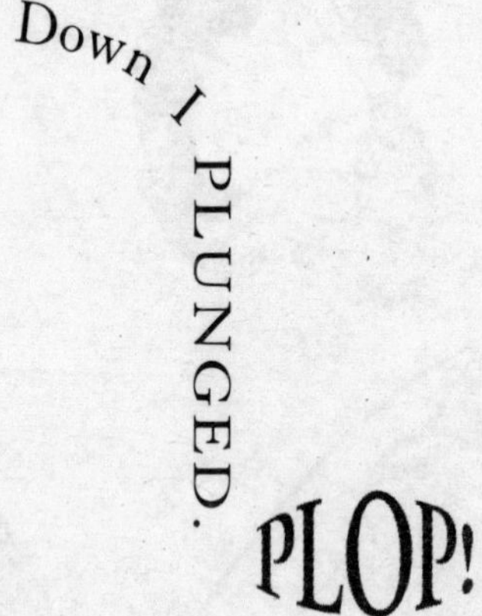

I landed on his back. It was surprisingly soft – like flopping on to a warm, squashy bed – except that Rory was moving beneath me as he leapt forward to follow the man with the beard.

"Slow down, Rory," called the man as we drew level with him. "Wait for me."

But the lion thundered past, bounding up the hill at TOP SPEED. I grabbed hold of a handful of mane and clung on tight.

CHAPTER 18

Riding a lion is one of the most exciting things I have ever done.

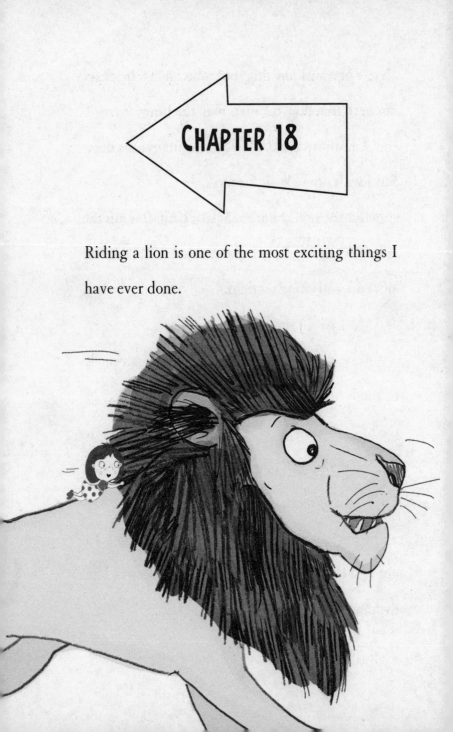

As Rory galloped, I could feel the muscles on his neck rippling beneath me. Looking down, I could see the grass flying past under his huge soft feet.

I love shrinking! I thought to myself. *One minute you think you're going to be eaten alive . . . but the next you're enjoying the ride of your life.*

"Giddy-up!" I cried.

Rory swerved sideways and leapt upwards through a thicket of trees, out on to the top of the hill.

Suddenly, it didn't look like we were in England any more.

There was a huge circle of clear ground spread out up here. Everything was dry and yellow – like the sandpit at King's Park.

About ten or fifteen people were scurrying around, busy with jobs. A man with a spade was widening the circle, sprinkling sand over tufts of green grass at the edge of the ring. Another was burning the leaves off a small bush with a fiery flame gun.

What was this place? It looked like . . . like *Africa*! What was going on?

As soon as they saw Rory, everyone looked up. But they didn't seem surprised to see a lion – after one quick glance, they were back to work.

I spotted Stella Lightfoot standing beside the cameraman I'd seen by the limousine earlier.

She took a step forward with her hands in the air.

"**Mr Arkmann,**" she bellowed. "**Mr Arkmann, where are you?**"

Rory had slowed to a trot now and the man with the bushy yellow beard came running up the hill behind us.

"Sorry, Miss Lightfoot," he panted, wiping his brow. He grabbed Rory by the mane as I ducked under a shaggy tuft of fur.

"This naughty lion's been giving me the run-around," he puffed.

"Let's just get started," ordered Stella. "I'd like to be finished in time for a late lunch. I want to make something nice. Maybe an omelette. . ."

An omelette? Why was Stella Lightfoot thinking about cooking when there was a lion breathing down her neck (even if he didn't seem to be a very dangerous one)?

Rory was right beside her now. We were so

close, I could have jumped off his neck and into the pocket of Stella's purple-and-black jumpsuit if I'd wanted to.

"Get on with it, everybody," she said, clapping her hands. "You've all got plenty of work to do."

The more I saw of Stella Lightfoot, the less I liked her. In real life, she was nothing like she seemed on TV. She was so **BOSSY** and **SNAPPY**, always shouting at everyone.

From my spot on Rory's back, I could see Pete the driver, dozing in the shade of a tree.

I remembered how Stella had shouted at him when he picked her up from the

this morning. That was when things first seemed strange. Why hadn't she been camping like she said she would? She'd stayed at the smart hotel with its gold doors and fancy French chef. Nothing made any sense.

Most of all, I had no idea what we were doing on top of a hill in the middle of England, with a circle of sand, a big tame lion and a man burning the leaves off a bush. It was obvious Stella Lightfoot was making a film here. But why?

The next twenty minutes were a **BUZZ** of action. The man with the spade piled up heaps of sand that looked like giant anthills. The flame-gun guy burnt the leaves off yet another bush. The cameraman kept squinting at the sun and moving his camera from one position to another. Even Pete the driver was set to work, rolling a big rock to the edge of the sand.

"You have to wait here until I am finished, anyway," said Stella. "You might as well make yourself useful."

At least that meant Pete wasn't about to drive away without me.

As Stella bellowed orders at everyone, they ran in all directions across the sand. The only person who seemed calm was Mr Arkmann. He sat at the edge of the circle stroking Rory's ears. The huge lion lay with his head in his owner's lap, as if he were a pet dog like Chip rather than a wild African beast or the King of the Jungle.

Still, I remembered the view I'd had of his

ENORMOUS teeth.

I kept well away from Rory's dangerous jaws, tucked round the back of his neck, where Mr Arkmann couldn't see me. I could have easily have jumped down and scampered off. But this was the perfect place to watch everything and find out what was going on. And while I was on Rory's back, he definitely couldn't eat me.

I peered out from under his **thick mane**. So long as I stayed tiny, no one would ever guess I was here. I tried not to think about what would happen if I suddenly grew back to **FULL SIZE**. How would I explain to Stella Lightfoot where I had come from? Or to Pete? As far as he knew, he had dropped me by the library in town.

Oh dear. I thought about Gran again. At least

my text had told her I was safe. She'd love to hear how I'd ridden a lion. I just needed to get home in one piece so that I could tell her about it.

"Ready now, Mr Arkmann," called a man with a clipboard. I think he must have been the director. "We're about to start filming."

Mr Arkmann stood up and clicked his fingers.

In an instant, Rory was on his feet. His whole body SHUDDERED. The hair bristled on the back of his neck. The tame pet was gone. This was a WILD BEAST.

ROOOOOAAAAAARRRRR!

He opened his mouth and bellowed. The people on the sand scuttled out of the way.

Only Stella Lightfoot was left now. I was sure I had seen her over by the trees a moment earlier but now she was standing all alone in the middle of the ring. She stood with her back towards us, wearing her purple-and-black CAMOUFLAGE jumpsuit. Her blonde ponytail was blowing in the breeze.

Rory thundered forward.

"Stop!" I cried helplessly as he leapt into the air. Had he gone mad? He had suddenly turned savage.

Rory's paws thumped against Stella Lightfoot's back, knocking her to the ground.

"Stop it!" I screamed, tugging on his hair as he pounced on top of her.

He was going to kill her. Why was nobody helping?

For a moment I couldn't see anything. Just a

frenzy of fur and claws – flying legs and arms – as the lion fought with the body beneath him.

"That'll do," said a voice beside me.

Then, just as quickly as it had started, I felt Rory relax.

I looked up to see Stella Lightfoot standing at Rory's shoulder.

But how was that possible?

I looked down. If Stella was standing beside us, then who was the body lying motionless on the ground?

Stella Lightfoot looked down at the ripped shape, lying still on the sand.

I hid under Rory's mane, my heart **pounding** like a drum.

Stella nudged the body with her toe.

"Get up, Anne," she barked. "We haven't got all day."

"Sorry," mumbled the body, and she sat up.

She didn't seem hurt. Perhaps Rory had been playing after all. But who was this person? I'd thought she was Stella Lightfoot when I had seen her standing alone in the middle of the ring – but her name seemed to be *Anne*. She staggered to her feet and brushed herself down.

As she turned, I saw her face for the first time.

"Huh?" I gasped. "What. . .?"

Anne's face was the same as Stella's. Exactly the same. The same green eyes. The same smooth blonde fringe. The same small turned-up nose. How could that be?

Unless. . . I thought of Cora and Dora, two old ladies who live at the same retirement centre as Gran. TWINS! Mum can never tell them apart and I always have to whisper their names to help her out when she's talking to them. It's actually really easy to tell the difference between them.

Cora has freckles on her nose like me and Dora doesn't. But nobody ever seems to notice that.

I glanced from Stella to Anne. They were almost identical – except Anne had a tiny scar above her lip.

"Was that all right, Stell?" she asked nervously. She picked a twig out of her hair. I suddenly remembered where I had seen that long, swishy ponytail – exactly like Stella's – before.

The woman in the cap outside Pages Bookshop. . . She'd handed Stella the big felt-tip pen to sign my mermaid tail. I remembered how I'd noticed her dark glasses. It seemed Anne didn't want the public to know she was Stella's twin.

"We've got some great footage," said the director

with the clipboard. "You did brilliantly, Anne."

"Yeah, but we've still got a tiger to film, or something," huffed Stella, raising her eyebrows in exactly the same way Tiff does when Mum's praising me.

"Not a tiger," sighed Anne. And I knew that sound. It's the same sigh I use when Tiff gets confused between a bulldog and a basset hound. Or thinks kick boxing and kung fu are the same thing. "We're supposed to be on safari. Tigers don't live in Africa. They live in India, silly."

"Whatever!" said Stella, *exactly* like Tiff would say it.

These two definitely must be sisters, I thought.

"Good boy, Rory," said Anne, tickling the lion's nose. "You were wonderful. Anyone would believe you really were going to eat me alive."

I crouched under Rory's mane as Anne rubbed his ears – her hands were just a few centimetres away from me. Rory made a soft PURRING noise and stretched his neck.

Anne turned and smiled at Mr Arkmann. "Thank you for letting us film him, Mr A. How's your wife? And the baby?"

"Tip-top, thank you," grinned Mr Arkmann, a red blush creeping up from under his beard. "Mrs A made a pot of jam for you actually. Fresh rhubarb, from the garden. She made one for Stella too."

"Really?" grinned Stella. It was only about the second time since I had seen her in real life that she'd smiled properly – like she usually does on telly. It was strange. Why should a pot of jam make her look so happy?

"I would love to try and make some for myself," she said, still smiling. "The gooseberry jelly you brought me last time was amazing."

"Careful," laughed Anne. "Stella will be after the recipe next."

Perhaps Gran was right – like she had said when we found all the kitchen things in the make-up bag. Stella must be a **really keen cook**.

Anne tickled Rory under the chin. But Stella glanced at her watch.

"Look at the time," she thundered, all the joy gone from her face again. "Get that lion out of here. Will someone fetch whatever stupid creature we're supposed to see next?"

Stupid creature? The Stella Lightfoot I'd seen on television was animal-crazy!

The director looked at his clipboard.

"We need the giraffe," he called.

Giraffe? It was like a zoo round here. I stood

up on tiptoes, trying to see. But Anne flung her arms around Rory's neck.

"Goodbye," she said.

As she hugged the lion, her elbow knocked me off his mane and sent me flying through the air.

I landed on the soft sand and rolled over in a ball as Mr Arkmann led Rory away.

Right beside me, I spotted a single green leaf. It must have fallen off the bush before the flame-gun guy had a chance to burn it. I scuttled underneath it, as secret as a beetle in a garden.

Peeping out, I could see the burnt bush beside me. With its blackened charcoal twigs, it looked like a thorn tree – the sort of thing you'd find growing on the African plains.

If I didn't know better, I would actually have

believed I was in the middle of an African game reserve. Although really, it was nothing but sand and tame lions.

I peeped out from the other side of the leaf, just in time to see a tall giraffe step daintily into the African scene.

"Good girl, Twiggy," said Mr Arkmann.

"Wow!" I gasped, craning my neck to look upwards. Twiggy was beautiful – the TALLEST giraffe I'd ever seen (maybe it was just because I was so tiny, but she towered above me like an elegant, dainty dinosaur).

As she came closer, I couldn't see the top of her head any more. Just her speckled tummy . . . then her long legs . . . her dry, cracked knees . . . her spotty ankles . . . her hooves . . . and. . .

"Yikes!"

Something long and black and slimy shot out towards me.

"Help!" Twiggy's thick, wet tongue wrapped itself around my tummy as she slurped up the fresh green leaf that I was hiding under. She had found the only thing to eat in the entire ring of sand.

Chapter 20

"Help! Put me down!" I squealed as the giraffe lifted her head.

In less than a second, she would eat the leaf and I would disappear with it down her long, long, long, long throat.

I flung myself into the air as the giraffe flicked her slippery tongue round the side of her face. I read once that giraffes' tongues are so long they can lick their own ears.

For a split second I saw the mile-high drop to the ground beneath me – as if I were leaping from a crane. My dress spread out like a parachute. Then I felt the tips of my fingers grab hold of a soft tuft of fur.

I was safe. I was clinging on to Twiggy's hairy earlobe, dangling like a purple polka-dot earring.

I swung my legs up and clutched one of the stubby horns right on the top of her head – hugging it tight.

Below me, Twiggy opened her mouth and swallowed the leaf.

"Phew!" I could feel the panic fluttering in my chest like a butterfly in a jar.

"That was a close one," I shuddered. "Too close!"

As my breathing steadied, I looked around me.

"Wow!" The view from up here was incredible. It was as if Twiggy was a giant flagpole right on top of the hill and I was standing on the very tip.

It seemed funny to see the green English countryside stretching away beyond the dry sand circle.

If I looked up, I felt as if I could almost touch the fluffy white clouds.

I could hear Stella Lightfoot shouting on the sand behind us.

"Get that wretched giraffe out of the way, Mr Arkmann. I need to do my introduction first," she roared.

Mr Arkmann led Twiggy towards the same thicket of trees I had charged through when I was riding Rory.

I clung tight to her horn.

"Welcome to **EXPLORE GALORE!**," I heard Stella say to the camera. Her voice sounded light and breezy now. "Here I am in search of the world's tallest animal. . ."

"You stay here and nibble some leaves, Twiggy," whispered Mr Arkmann, patting her neck. "I'm just going to make sure Rory gets a drink of water."

Twiggy stretched her head up through the branches. As I watched Mr Arkmann hurry away, I had a brainwave.

I could slide all the way down Twiggy's neck. . .

I was so small, I wouldn't hurt her – but her **SMOOTH** hair would be like a slippery shoot . . . like the longest, fastest, coolest slide imaginable. Something only someone as tiny as me could ever ride on.

Once I was at the bottom of her neck, I could scramble across her back and shimmy down her leg somehow. Then I could hide in amongst the trees while I decided what to do next. No one would discover me there. I had been shrunk for ages – surely it wouldn't be long before I grew back to full size.

"Here goes," I whispered, staring down the long speckled slope beneath me. "**This is SO cool!**"

I edged forward and hitched up my dress.

This would be SO much easier if I were wearing shorts, I thought.

I sat myself down just to the left of Twiggy's stubby mane. That way I'd have a smooth path down her neck – but I could still grab a clump of hair if I felt as if I was going to fall.

I slithered forward and lifted my feet so they wouldn't drag and slow me down.

"Geronimo!" I cried.

Away I slid – facing forward, as if I was on a slide.

D
o
w
n
I flew.

My dress was flapping around my face. It was awesome with the wind whistling past my ears – like the tallest, craziest, living, breathing helter-skelter in the world.

My ears popped. My stomach lurched. It felt as if there was popcorn exploding inside me as I dropped down and. . .

"Oh no!" I knew that feeling.

I just had time to flip over as I shot off the end of Twiggy's neck and landed **FULL SIZE** on her back.

At least I was facing the right way.

Twiggy skittered sideways and charged out of the trees.

Now I was full size she knew she had a rider. She twisted her hind legs like a corkscrew, kicking them in the air and bucking like a wild horse.

"Steady," I breathed, clinging on to her neck and trying to pat her at the same time.

Everyone could see us now.

Mr Arkmann sprinted across the sand.

"Whoa," he coaxed.

"Careful," gasped Anne, leaping forward.

"Stop!" screamed Stella Lightfoot, from in front of the camera. "Get off that giraffe. Right now!"

Getting down from a giraffe is not easy – even when you're **FULL SIZE**.

Mr Arkmann held Twiggy's head while the director and the flame-guy fetched a ladder and held it against her side.

My legs were wobbling as I climbed to the ground.

"Who are you?" frowned the director.

"What are you doing here?" growled a man with a spade.

Only the cameraman was smiling.

"That was stunning. I managed to film you riding," he said.

"What I don't understand is how you got up there in the first place, young lady," said Mr Arkmann, scratching his beard.

"I-I was in the trees over there," I said, pointing to the little wood. "I sort of . . . fell on to her back from above."

That was true – in a way.

"Hold on. I know you," said Pete the driver, pointing at me. "You're the kid who was in my limousine this morning." He turned towards the director. "She disappeared all of a sudden. Her gran said she'd gone to the library but she must have hidden in the car."

"A SPY," said Stella Lightfoot.

"Gran!" I gasped at the same time. It was ages since I'd sent my text. I needed to let her know I was safely back to full size. I turned to Stella, who was staring at me with her hands on her hips.

"I promise I am not a spy. I'm here by accident," I said. "But please, can I borrow your phone? I need to let my family know I'm all right."

"Fine," sighed Stella. "Make a call. But you'd better have some answers when you're done. This is a private film location. I want to know what you are doing here and. . . Wait a minute. . ." She stepped closer and peered into my face. "I know you as well."

"Really?" I asked. The last time Stella had seen me, I had been dressed as a mermaid with green glitter all over my face.

"You're the girl who was wearing the fish suit," she said.

"Mermaid," I corrected.

"Your name is Vera, isn't it?

"Violet," I said.

"Whatever. They filmed us outside the book shop," said Stella. "It made the local news. I would recognize that wobbly fringe anywhere."

My fingers shot up to my forehead, feeling the gap where Rosie had made such a mess of cutting my hair.

"Sorry. I really do need to phone my gran," I said.

I wasn't sure what else I could say.

CHAPTER 22

By the time I had finished my phone call, and convinced Gran that I was full size and safe, the film crew had stopped for lunch.

Stella Lightfoot had set up a little gas camping stove for herself. She was standing beside it, warming butter in a frying pan as the flames flickered blue and orange.

My stomach RUMBLED. I hadn't eaten anything for hours – not since the pink wafer biscuits with Gran.

I edged closer to the stove.

I was determined to speak to Stella – even if that meant answering some really awkward questions.

This is my last chance, I thought. *I have to convince her to help save Mo's café.*

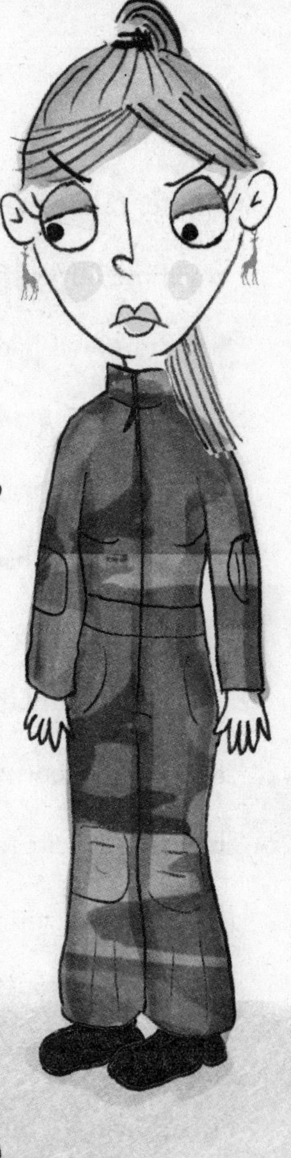

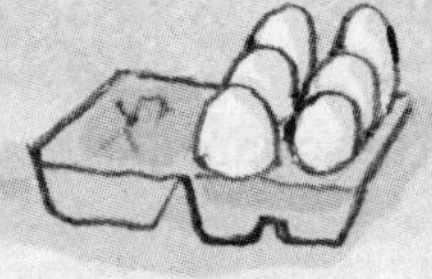

I had ridden a lion . . . and slid off a towering giraffe. Talking to an **angry** celebrity couldn't be any more difficult than that. Could it?

But now I had met her properly, I wasn't sure that Stella *would* help us. I wasn't even sure that she *could*.

As I gave back her phone, my hands were shaking.

Talking to Gran had given me time to think. Stella Lightfoot wanted me to answer questions, but there were a lot of things she needed to explain too.

"I know you were going to film the giraffe," I said. "I saw you already with the lion."

"Really?" Stella's eyelid twitched, but she didn't look up as she cracked an egg into a bowl.

"Yes," I said. "And I know about your sister." I glanced round. There was no sign of Anne anywhere. Somebody had probably told her to hide so that I wouldn't be able to get a good look at her. As soon as I started to speak, I realized I knew exactly what was going on.

"I know she's your twin," I said. "I know she does all the scary stunts for you. All the DANGEROUS bits, like being attacked by a lion. Although Rory's tame anyway. He's been specially trained. I know you are pretending this is Africa – as if you have really gone there on safari." I could hear my voice going high and SQUEAKY as I pointed to the sand circle. I hadn't realized I was so angry. But I loved EXPLORE GALORE! and now I had found out that none of it was real.

"You just get a man with a flame gun to burn the trees to make them look dry and hot," I said. Stella was beating the egg with a fork now, round and round and round. It didn't look as if she was even listening to me.

"You pretend to love animals but you call them stupid," I said. "You pretend to be wild and daring but you're not. You told everyone you were going to camp out last night, but you didn't. You stayed in a posh hotel with a fancy French chef!" My lip was trembling now.

"Swiss," sighed Stella, looking up at last. "The chef is Swiss. His speciality is cooking dishes with cheese."

I couldn't believe Stella was admitting it.

"Dare to dream – make your dreams happen,

whatever your dreams may be," I quoted. "That's what you say on **EXPLORE GALORE!**. But none of it is true. It's all fake."

My finger was shaking as I pointed at Stella Lightfoot.

"You're a fake," I said, my voice cracking as I spoke. "*A TOTAL FAKE*."

"All right! That's enough." I felt a hand on my shoulder. I turned to see Anne standing right behind me. Twiggy and Rory were with her – like two giant dogs following at heel.

"The truth is, I am the one who's a fake," she said, rubbing Rory's head. Twiggy nodded her long neck as if to agree. "Stella has tried to be truthful and honest. But it's all my fault. It is me who has tricked everyone."

Anne's hands were shaking even worse than mine.

"Be quiet, Anne." Stella slammed down the bowl of eggs. She shook her head and glared at me. "We don't have to tell this girl anything."

"But I've worked it out already," I said. "Anne makes the films, not you." I couldn't believe Stella was still going to deny what was happening. "She's the BRAVE one. She's the one who stood there and was attacked by a lion."

"Stell, we can't keep on pretending," said Anne. "Violet here has seen far too much. Perhaps it will be for the best. We can put an end to all this." She pointed to the sand and the burnt bushes. "Neither of us wants to go on with the lies."

"But she's just a nosey kid." Stella shook her

wooden spoon at me. "You can't ruin this," she hissed. "Not after Anne has worked so hard. I won't let you."

She sloshed the egg mixture into the sizzling pan and it spat angrily as it hit the heat.

"Come on," said Anne, taking me by the arm. "Let's leave Stella to cook. And I'll tell you everything. The whole truth. I promise."

CHAPTER 23

Anne and I sat down under a tree and Mr Arkmann joined us.

Rory lay down behind us and we leant against him like a HUGE SOFT sofa. Twiggy rested her head lovingly on Anne's shoulder.

We could still see Stella at the camping stove, crashing around among the pans. It was clear she was in a FURIOUS mood.

"Don't worry, she'll calm down," said Mr Arkmann.

"Always does when she's cooking," agreed Anne.

It was funny, sitting here talking to someone who looked exactly like Stella Lightfoot –someone who was the spitting image of a famous celebrity. But the minute Anne started to speak, I could tell she was different. Stella always held her head high. Anne sort of ducked whenever she was talking. Stella's voice was **loud**. Anne's was quiet.

But the main difference was the way Anne was around the animals.

"You really do love them, don't you?" I said, as she reached up and stroked Twiggy's neck. Rory was purring like a big tomcat.

"I'm animal-CRAZY. Always have been," said Anne. "That's how all this started. I got a job making a television show about them. It was the first series of **EXPLORE GALORE!**. The film crew all flew out to the Amazon rainforest."

"I remember that," I said. "The one where Stella went down the river in a tree-trunk canoe?"

"Stella? In a canoe?" Mr Arkmann laughed. "You mean the one where *Anne* went down the river. Stella can barely swim. She hates water."

"She'd be scared to death that a crocodile would nip her toes," smiled Anne.

"Truth is," sighed Mr Arkmann, "Stella's hopeless at all that wild and daring stuff. . ."

"And I love it," said Anne. "But I am hopeless at talking to a camera." She was chewing her nails. "As soon as anyone starts filming, I just sort of clam up. That first time, in the Amazon jungle . . . they knew I was a disaster on day one."

"But they had already flown everyone out there," said Mr Arkmann. "It was so expensive.

They had to find a way to make the film."

"Every time I tried to speak, I practically burst into tears," said Anne. "I phoned Stella and she said she would help me. She was about to go to cookery college and train to be a chef, but she had done some acting at school. She's **BRILLIANT** at it. I convinced the film company that nobody would be able to tell the difference between us. Then we filmed all the scary stuff without me saying a word. When we came back from the Amazon, we just added Stella's voiceover in a studio. We shot a few extra scenes with a friendly crocodile so we could link up with the footage I'd already filmed in the wild."

"Snapper," laughed Mr Arkmann. "Lovely old croc he was. I run a small private zoo, rescuing mistreated circus animals and that sort of thing. I can always find any tame ones we need."

"But most of the filming is real . . . all the stuff in the wild," said Anne. "I promise. It's just me that you see doing it. Not Stella."

"Like now," nodded Mr Arkmann. "Anne has already filmed everything in Africa for the safari series. We're just shooting some last little bits, so that Stella can add the voiceover and make it look as if she was really with the animals."

"But I don't understand. You're so BRAVE," I said, looking at Anne. "I've seen the things you do: running with wolves; deep-sea diving in shark-infested water. I saw you today, when Rory attacked you. I know he's trained, but it still must have been scary. . ."

"Oh, that's easy!" said Anne. "I'd rather put my head inside a lion's mouth than say lines to a camera or meet the public. Stella is the brave one, really. She does all the talking – she's the real celebrity who goes to all the book signings and things. She's the one who has made the show a HUGE success."

Anne was still biting her fingernails. "I think it takes far more guts to appear in front of an audience than to swim with a great white shark," she said quietly.

"I suppose so," I agreed. I could sort of understand what she meant. I thought about all the daring things I have done when I've shrunk – things that people would say were brave – rolling down the stairs in a Russian doll, riding a lion, sliding down a giraffe's neck. I didn't really think of them as scary – I love the excitement too much.

"Different things seem brave to different people," said Mr Arkmann. "With me it's heights. I can't even climb a ladder."

"But that's the problem," said Anne. "Stella saved the show. **EXPLORE GALORE!** was a huge hit. We thought it would just be for that first episode. But I had signed a contract – they wouldn't let us stop. Stella has to appear on chat shows. Meet fans. It never ends."

"We've made five series now," explained Mr Arkmann.

"And Stella never got to go to cookery school," said Anne. "Even though it's the thing she really loves."

I looked over towards Stella again. She did seem calmer now that she was cooking. She had served all the film crew with steaming hot omelettes and was beating more eggs in a bowl.

"She's a good person," nodded Mr Arkmann. "She's done all this for her twin sister."

"And she's not really GRUMPY and CROSS like you've seen her," said Anne. "That's just the stress of all the lies we have to tell. Imagine always having to pretend to be someone else. Never being able to be yourself."

"Violet!" Stella's voice boomed across the film set. "Come here."

"She is *very* bossy though," laughed Anne. "That's sisters for you."

"What does she want me for?" I gulped,

clambering to my feet.

"She won't bite," smiled Anne.

"And if she does, punch her on the nose," grinned Mr Arkmann. "That's a trick I learnt from fighting crocodiles."

As I walked across the sand, Stella was shaking her wooden spoon at me again.

"I suppose you don't want an omelette," she said.

Omelettes really aren't my favourite food – especially the spinach ones Mum makes – but I didn't dare say no.

"An omelette would be . . . nice," I lied.

"Really?" Stella raised her eyebrows. "I thought you'd rather have pancakes. I've whipped up some cream. And I've got some toppings here somewhere." She unzipped her CAMOUFLAGE bag and pulled out the three little pots of sprinkles.

"Chocolate chips shaped like sharks, hundreds and thousands, or would you prefer crunchy stars?" she grinned. Her smile was a totally proper one – even bigger than when she was speaking on EXPLORE GALORE!, or posing for the news camera the day before.

"Chocolate sharks, of course," I said. "I love pancakes."

Stella showed me how to make batter and we

tossed the pancakes in the air.

I dropped one on the ground – it had that same **gritty** look I had when I fell out of Nisha's pocket in the King's Park sandpit.

"Don't worry. Rory will eat that," said Stella. "But you have to hold the pan flatter. No! Not like that. Like this!"

Anne was right – Stella *was* bossy . . . but she wasn't horrible. Not like the person I had seen on the film set or in the limo. As soon as she was cooking, she was different.

We made pancakes for Anne and Mr Arkmann too, and we all ate them leaning against Rory, with Twiggy resting her neck on our heads.

"Yum. This is **scrumdiddilyumptious!**" I said, taking a huge mouthful of pancake, fresh cream and chocolatey shark-shaped sprinkles.

"Everything Stella makes is always scrumdiddilyumptious," smiled Anne

"That's because cooking makes me happy,"

said Stella. But she didn't look happy. As I glanced over, I saw that her eyes were full of tears.

I couldn't bear to think of her so sad. I'd always imagined Stella Lightfoot fearlessly fighting sharks and smiling as she escaped from a charging bull. But this was the *real* Stella – not someone I imagined I knew just because I'd seen her on TV. I thought how awful it must be to spend so much time never being able to do what you want.

"Why don't you do a show about cooking instead of all this?" I said, waving towards the burnt bushes and the pretend anthills in the sand.

"I wish I could," sighed Stella.

"But you can," I said. Everything seemed so simple to me, I couldn't understand why Stella and Anne couldn't see it. "It's like you say on

EXPLORE GALORE! – *whichever* one of you it is who says it, it doesn't matter: *Dare to dream – make your dreams happen, whatever your dreams may be!*"

Stella laughed.

"That's just a silly line we say in the show," said Anne. "Stella can't follow her dreams – not really. She's forced to go on pretending to jump off waterfalls and fight wild animals. She's forced to go on pretending that she is me."

"And so neither of us is happy," sighed Stella. "We HATE all the lies. I am always so grumpy and cross. Anne bites her nails and hardly sleeps a wink at night."

"I'm sorry, Violet." Anne leant over and touched my hand as I was about to lift my fork for another bite of pancake. "You must be very disappointed in us. But at least now you know the truth."

"I suppose you'll go to the newspapers and tell them everything," said Stella, staring down at her plate.

"No." I shook my head gently so as not to wake the animals. Rory was snoring loudly behind me. Twiggy had drifted off to sleep with her chin on my shoulder. "I'm not going to tell the papers anything," I said. "But, if you'll let me help you, I do have a plan. Do you think the television company might let you make two programmes instead of one?"

"Two programmes?" groaned Anne. "Why on earth would we want to do that?"

Twiggy's head shot up in the air. Rory growled in his sleep.

"Even more lies," sighed Stella.

"No. It's not about telling lies," I said. "I think I know a way that both your dreams can come true. But you have to help me too . . . and my friend Mo, the one I tried to tell you about.

She has a dream of her own. . ."

Anne and Stella both came to Swanchester in the limo when Pete brought me back that afternoon. I phoned Gran and told her to meet us at the hairdresser so that I could get my fringe cut before Mum saw that it was still wonky.

Anne came into the salon with me.

"I'd like a haircut just like hers," she said, pointing at me. "A short fringe and neat round the back."

She leant over and whispered in my ear, "It'll be much easier to keep tidy when I'm camping in the jungle. . . And I won't look like Stella any more."

In the end, it was the haircut that helped convince the television company to scrap **EXPLORE GALORE!**. Stella refused to cut her hair short and Anne refused to ever grow hers again. Now they could no longer pretend to be the same person.

"I want to make a series about **FOOD**," Stella told the company.

"And I'll happily make a brand-new programme about animals and adventure," said Anne. "But I am not going to speak a single word. I will be in disguise. A **MYSTERY** presenter. No one will even know who I am."

So that is what they did, and I was there to help them. Rather than filming any more episodes of **EXPLORE GALORE!** the television company made two completely new shows instead.

We started work on the first one almost immediately. After all, there was no time to lose – not if I wanted to help Mo.

The series was called **DREAM CUISINE** and it was all about food. The idea was simple.

Stella Lightfoot went to visit great cafes and restaurants. She talked live to the chefs about their favourite recipes, and then she had a go at making them herself – right there in their kitchens.

"This is a *real* adventure," Stella laughed, talking straight to the camera.

I was sitting on a stool watching her film. Instead of her familiar CAMOUFLAGE, she was wearing an apron covered in bunches of bright **black** and **purple** grapes.

"I always dreamed of going to cookery school," she said as the camera followed her. "But this is even better. I get to learn how to make brilliant food with true professionals."

"I don't know about professionals," replied Mo, coming into shot. Of course, we had chosen

UDDERLY PERFECT as the very first place to film. "I taught myself how to cook," she said. "But I do know that if you want to make that milkshake taste really **thick** and fruity, you're going to need to add another big handful of fresh strawberries and some banana too."

While Stella was filming at UDDERLY PERFECT, she signed our petition and recorded interviews with local people saying the café was part of the community – much more important than a multi-storey car park.

When the council heard this, they agreed to give the café a second chance and inspect it again. They said that the accident with the milkshake could have happened anywhere. Mr Zeal was sent away to retrain.

On the day he came back to visit UDDERLY PERFECT again, we were just finishing filming. The director spotted him at once.

"Would you talk to the camera?" he said.

"This café is exceptionally clean and safe," droned Mr Zeal, in a flat voice. "No bacteria or germs have been identified. I can find no reason that fresh food and beverages should not be served here. Providing, of course, that all spillages are mopped up with due care."

Nisha was with me and we both collapsed with LAUGHTER. We were sure Mr Zeal was being funny. But he didn't even smile.

"Perfect!" said the director, jumping up from his chair. "You're a real star, Mr Zeal. A natural."

Sure enough, the public loved Mr Zeal, with his straight face and serious voice. You can even buy mugs and aprons saying **MR ZEAL HAS INSPECTED MY KITCHEN – IT IS CLEAN AND SAFE**. He has become Health and Safety Advisor for the whole series now, visiting every restaurant and café where **DREAM CUISINE** goes.

But, best of all, he presented Mo with a certificate saying **UDDERLY PERFECT** could stay open for business.

As soon as his inspection was over and Stella and the film crew had gone home, Mo threw her arms around me.

"Thank you, Violet. You saved the café," she beamed.

"I couldn't have done it without Anne and Stella's help," I said. "Now the café is ***FAMOUS***, there's no way the council can close it down."

I pointed to a smiling, signed photograph of Stella on the wall.

"Both the twins are happy now there's no more **EXPLORE GALORE!**," I said. "Whenever I see Stella cooking or talking about food, she really does grin. Properly. Just like in that photo."

Congratulations on such an Udderly Perfect café! Thank you for sharing your recipes! Love, Stella x, it said.

"And I have just the thing to put up beside it," chuckled Mo, slipping the Health and Safety certificate into a gold frame. **UDDERLY PERFECT** had been awarded five stars.

"Look," I giggled. "It's even signed by Mr Zeal. Perhaps you should get a photo of him as well."

The second TV series we made is called WILD CHILD . . . and it stars Anne Lightfoot. Though, just as we planned, nobody knows it's her – she's like a mystery adventurer. There is no blonde ponytail any more, of course. Anne appears in a black suit with a face mask. She has lots of different suits – a stretchy one for climbing, a waterproof one for swimming and an extra-thick one for skiing. They call her the Cat Explorer. She does all the stunts herself, but nobody ever knows who she is, because she doesn't say a word.

That's the whole point of WILD CHILD.

Have you seen it? Different kids appear on the show each week. They are the presenters – they do all the talking. Anne does all the really **DANGEROUS** stuff – the sorts of things parents would never let their children do. Things like putting their heads inside a crocodile's mouth. But the children still get to meet the animals and explain what's going on.

"In the first episode I'm going to be swimming with dolphins off the coast of Wales," Anne told me over the phone. "Do you know any kids who could help us? Someone who'd like to splash about like a mermaid perhaps?"

"How about Violet herself?" I heard Stella laughing in the background. "She'd make a **BRILLIANT** mermaid. She even has her own suit."

But I had a **MUCH** better idea than that.

"I know two girls who would be perfect," I said.

And that is how Nisha and Rosie got to be a little bit ***FAMOUS***, just like me.

"I can't believe I'm really here," said Nisha as we bobbed up and down in the sea. A family of dolphins swam round and round us – close enough so we could reach out and touch them.

"I love dolphins," squealed Rosie, splashing around beside us in a pair of big orange armbands so that she could stay afloat.

"We know you love dolphins," laughed Nisha. Rosie had told us this about a million times already.

Instead of her long blonde mermaid curls, Rosie still had short spiky hair from where she had cut it all off.

She looks like a little prickly sea urchin, I thought. But she was incredibly cute with her gappy-toothed smile, bobbing around in the water and blowing kisses to the dolphins.

I caught a glimpse of her *Patty Pocket* doll poking out above one armband. She was still wearing her tiny pink bikini. But since I had last seen her, *Patty's* beautiful long curls had been snipped away. She had short spiky hair just like Rosie's now.

I think I had a lucky escape, I chuckled to myself. *I'd rather face the jaws of a lion than a toddler with a pair of scissors.*

"I love dolphins," said Rosie again, swallowing a mouthful of sea water. "**I love dolphins. I love dolphins.**"

"Good," I giggled, pulling my snorkelling goggles further down over my face and paddling away. Rosie kept looking at me very strangely, as if she recognized me from somewhere. I didn't want her to think that Princess Tiny-Twinkle, her mini-mermaid doll, had come to life.

Markus, the same director who had worked on **EXPLORE GALORE!**, jumped into the water between us.

"We're about to start filming now," he said as Anne joined us. "When I say 'Ready', swim towards the camera. Rosie, you say how much you love dolphins. Nisha, you can tell the viewers that these are bottlenose dolphins, sometimes seen in waters off the UK."

"**I love dolphins!**" shouted Rosie at the top of her voice.

"Not quite yet," smiled Markus. "I'll tell you when we're ready."

"What about you, Violet?" asked Nisha, swimming back towards me. "Aren't you going to be filmed?"

"Not today. The dolphins are just for you and Rosie," I said. "I'm going to film next week. Anne is taking me diving in a cage to see sharks."

"But what if you shrink?" hissed Nisha. "You'll slip though the bars and the sharks will gobble you up like a mini sardine."

"Yikes! I hadn't thought of that," I said. "You'd better come with me and keep a look out, just in case."

"Me? With sharks?" Nisha didn't look so sure, but before she could say anything else, Markus waved in our direction.

"We're ready to film the dolphins now. Join in if you like, Violet," he said. "The more the merrier. But don't worry. We are definitely going to use that WILD and DARING film we shot of you riding the giraffe that time."

"Really?" A huge smile spread across my face. I couldn't believe I would be on telly doing such amazing things – riding a giraffe *and* swimming with sharks.

"I will be TOTALLY, TOTALLY FAMOUS!" I grinned.

I felt an excited tingling in the tips of my toes.

Oh no . . . I couldn't shrink. Not now. Not in the middle of the sea.

"I think I need to get back to the boat," I said, and I started to paddle as fast as I could. . .

Acknowledgements

A very BIG thank you to everyone at Scholastic. Especially Alice Swan for never SHRINKING from the editing task and Genevieve Herr for last minute MARVELS. Also to Alison Padley for her BRILLIANT design and Hannah Cooper and Sam Aaronberg for all the WONDERFUL publicity. To Kirsten Collier for TOTALLY FABULOUS illustrations. Also Pat White and Claire Wilson at RCW for all their help and support. And to Sophie McKenzie for reading and re-reading again!

Thanks also to my husband and children and all the people (like Maureen to whom this book is dedicated to) who have helped our family out in many different ways so that I can sneak away and write.

LOOK OUT
for Violet's other adventures

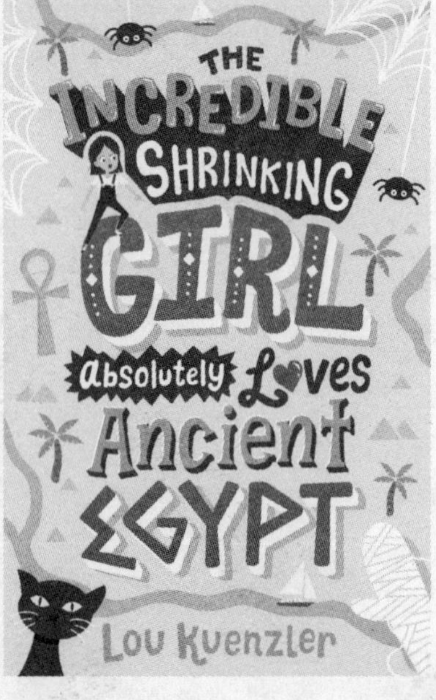

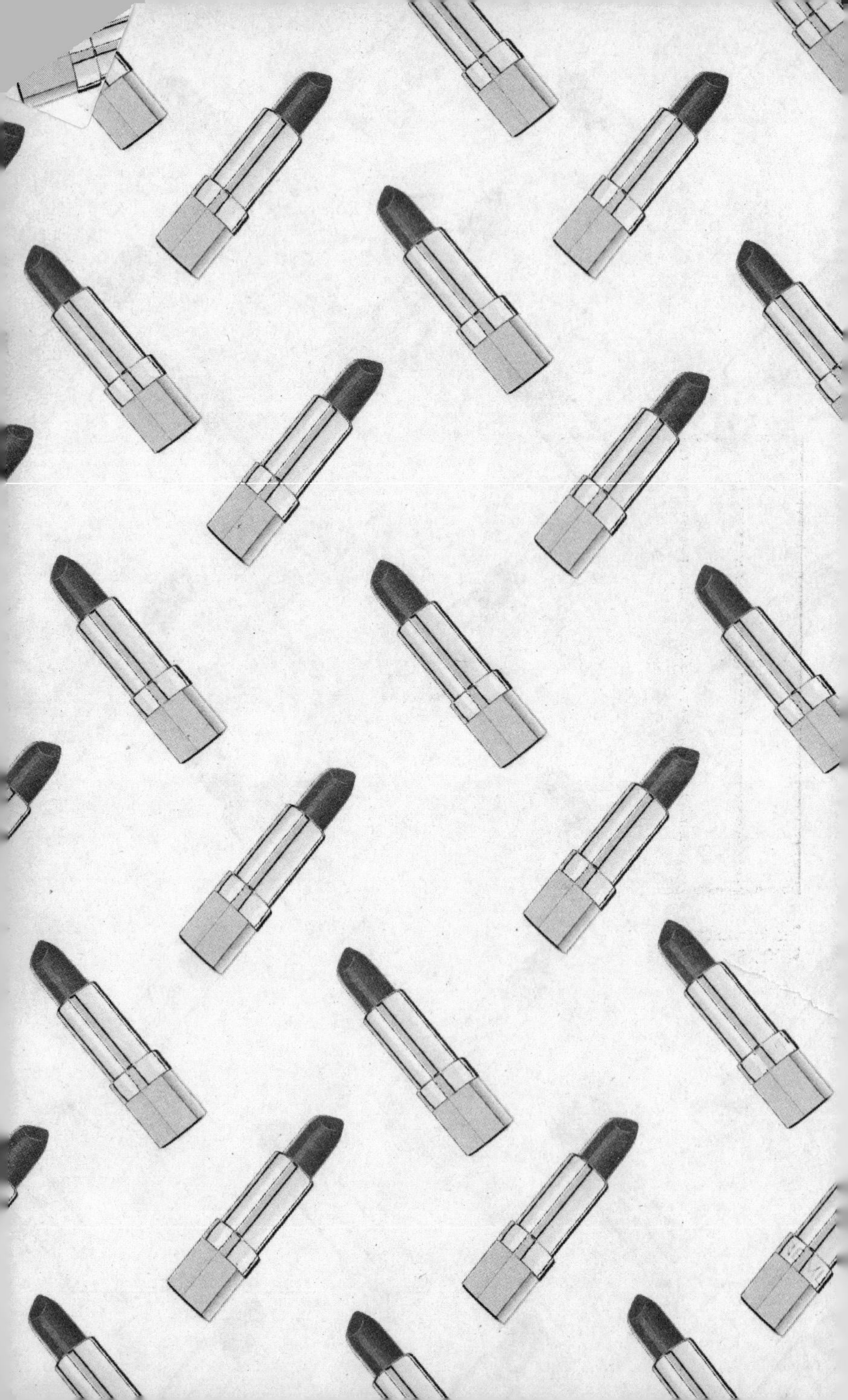